"I could be wrong but I think your cabin just blew up."

Ethan ran his fingers through his short hair. This was all *his* fault. He'd known there were people who held grudges. He'd read the anonymous letters.

Had one of them snapped?

She still hadn't said a word. He couldn't blame her. If he was right, she'd just lost something that had been in her family for generations. She would hate him when she learned the truth.

She slowly walked toward the door and looked past him. Smoke was continuing to billow up into the sky. Finally Chandler turned to him. Her eyes were dark with pain.

"I think I'm in trouble, Ethan. Real trouble."

HUNTED

—

BEVERLY LONG

For Beth and Wes Devenney,
who loved the mountains and me.

ISBN-13: 978-0-373-69780-9

HUNTED

Copyright © 2014 by Beverly R. Long

Printed in U.S.A.

ABOUT THE AUTHOR

As a child, Beverly Long used to take a flashlight to bed so that she could hide under the covers and read. Once a teenager, more often than not, the books she chose were romance novels. Now she gets to keep the light on as long as she wants, and there's always a romance novel on her nightstand. With both a bachelor's and a master's degree in business and more than twenty years of experience as a human resources director, she now enjoys the opportunity to write her own stories. She considers her books to be a great success if they compel the reader to stay up way past their bedtime.

Beverly loves to hear from readers. Visit www.beverlylong.com, or like her at www.facebook.com/beverlylong.romance.

Books by Beverly Long

CAST OF CHARACTERS

Chandler McCann—She's discovered that somebody at her work is selling military secrets to the enemy. Now men are trying to kill her. When she and Ethan Moore embark on a dangerous trek through the Colorado mountains, he promises to keep her safe. But is she an even bigger target when they're together?

Ethan Moore—He left the military under a heavy cloud of suspicion, and there are people who want him to pay for the crimes they believe he committed. Can he protect Chandler from danger, or is he the real reason somebody seems determined to harm her?

Marcus White—He's recently been upset at work. Is he so angry that he'd sell company secrets to the enemy and try to kill Chandler before she tells anyone?

Claudia Linder McCann—She's been Chandler's boss for years and only recently became her stepmother. Is it possible that this successful businesswoman is a traitor to her country? Or is she being duped by one of her employees?

Ted Matchmore—He blames Ethan Moore for his brother's death. Just how far is he willing to go to make sure that Ethan pays for what he's done?

Baker McCann—He was a single dad for a long time before falling for Claudia Linder. He can't believe what Chandler is saying about Claudia. Will he finally listen in time to save himself and his daughter?

Chapter One

Chandler McCann kept the radio on low since the thoughts in her head were making loud screeching sounds, spurring on a headache that no amount of diet soda could touch. All night, the headlights from oncoming traffic had seemed overly bright, catching sharp corners of the mammoth mountains, making them bulge and buckle in an unfriendly way, forcing her to hold the steering wheel in a viselike grip.

She was grateful to turn off the interstate, knowing that the cabin was now less than thirty minutes away. It had been two years since she'd been there. That time she'd gotten on the plane in Denver and the flight attendant barely had time to hand out beverages before the plane landed at the Eagle County Regional Airport fifty minutes later. The flight had been crowded with skiers headed toward Vail, which sat thirty miles to the east.

Mack had picked her up in his Jeep and they'd headed the opposite direction, winding their way through the mountains. With a carefree abandon that Chandler couldn't hope to imitate, her brother had navigated the string of razor-sharp switchbacks that, in many places, offered as little as a two-foot shoulder.

That day it had been sunny in the mountains. Tonight,

however, it had been dark for hours, and she'd been grateful for the half-moon that hung low in the sky. It would be after ten by the time she got to the cabin. It didn't matter. Nobody was expecting her.

She was supposed to be working. As always.

Certainly not running.

Ten minutes later, Chandler caught the glare of headlights coming toward her and clicked to low beams. The SUV passed and she caught a glimpse of two people in the front seat.

She took a sip of warm, flat soda and turned up the heat. She hadn't checked the weather but knew that it would be colder in the mountains than it had been in Denver. She suspected that she might regret not taking the time to pack a heavier jacket.

She slowed to take a curve, glanced in her rearview mirror and saw another set of car lights. She found some comfort in the fact that she wasn't alone out in the middle of nowhere. On the next curve, however, comfort turned to surprise when she realized the car behind her was gaining fast. The driver had to be flying, which was a dangerous thing on these roads.

Three minutes later, the vehicle was so close that the lights were blindingly bright. Who was crazy enough to tailgate here?

"Idiot," she muttered, just as the car bumped her.

She was so startled that it took her an extra second to react. She wrestled with the wheel. And was just bringing her car back under control when she was hit again. Her Toyota Camry skidded forward.

What the hell?

Once, an accident? Twice, no way. She pressed on the

gas, desperately wanting to put some space between her and the other car.

Then she got hit a third time. Hard.

Her car went airborne and her right front fender struck a glancing blow off the side of the mountain, sending her skidding across the narrow highway, straight toward the edge.

She slammed on the brakes. And started spinning.

She was going over.

And all she could do was hang on and wait to die.

When her car came to a stop, it was jarring. She pitched forward at the same time her air bag inflated.

It slapped her back in the seat, pushing hard against her face and chest. Her shoulder belt jerked tight. She felt a burning sensation arch across her cheekbones and settle on the bridge of her nose.

She stayed conscious, at least she thought she did, aware of the deflating air bag and the strong chemical smell it left behind. She also was aware that her neck hurt when she tried to turn her head.

Knew that she was in a hell of a mess.

But she was alive.

She had to get out. Now. It was the only thought in her head.

She fumbled to unclasp her seat belt. It sprang free and she pitched forward. It took effort to keep her spine pressed back against the seat.

Her car was upright but not level. No, definitely not. The front was way lower than the back.

She couldn't see much but what she could see wasn't encouraging. By some miracle, one of her headlights appeared to still be working. That, combined with the moonlight, allowed her to see that her windshield was cracked in multiple places and the front of her vehicle was badly damaged. She could feel the cool night air on the back of her neck. She turned her head, half expecting to see that the back of the car had been sheared off. But it was still intact, although the back window had been blown out.

And there were branches poking in.

Her car had somehow gotten hung up in the trees. She had no idea how far she'd fallen, how many times the car had rolled. She also had no idea of how much farther the car might tumble if it lost its perilous perch.

And that paralyzed her, until she finally forced herself to move. She carefully reached out and patted the seat next to her. Nothing. Her backpack, her purse and the cell phone that was in it had gotten tossed somewhere.

She extended her arm over the seat and waved it around, frantically hoping to hook a strap by some miracle. She could feel the car shift beneath her and heard the soft creak of a tree limb. She stopped, afraid to move, afraid to even breathe.

Out of the corner of her eye, she caught a patch of light. Bobbing and fading. Someone up on the road had a flashlight.

She wanted to weep with joy or scream for help. But she did neither.

She'd met only one vehicle. Minutes after it had passed, there had been someone following her.

Was it possible that the car had passed, realized it was her, turned around, and hurried to catch up? Then deliberately rammed into her. Three times.

What was the likelihood that they now wanted to help?

Deciding that playing dead was the best course of

action for the time being, she forced herself to slump over the steering wheel with her eyes closed.

She listened, knowing that voices carried in the night air.

It was quiet for several minutes. Finally, she heard a man say, "There. Happy? Now let's get the hell out of here."

There was a response, but it was too faint for her to distinguish the words. She couldn't even tell if it was a man or a woman.

"Oh, she's dead," the first man said, his voice booming with confidence. "Nobody could have survived that fall. Let's go."

Chandler heard the slam of two car doors. Then the sound of an engine starting. The noise faded as her attackers drove away.

She felt cold and battered and the urge to vomit came on with a vengeance. Someone had tried to kill her. The notion of it was so absolutely terrifying that her mind went blank.

But only for about ten seconds. Then she got furious. And determined.

Moving slowly and carefully, she leaned back in her seat. She took a deep breath, then another. The ability to think, to reason, started to come back as she flooded her brain with oxygen.

Nobody could have survived that fall.

She had. And from what she could tell, all her fingers and toes and all the parts in between were working.

Now she just needed to get out before the car took a final plunge.

ETHAN MOORE HAD just turned the last page of his book when he heard a noise that didn't belong to the quiet

Colorado countryside. He raised his eyes at the same moment his dog, Molly, raised her head. "What do you make of that, girl?"

Molly started to whine and turn circles on her rug.

"You just went out," he said. She did another circle.

The temperature had been dropping all day. What had started out as a pretty October morning had become a windy, cold night. Snow was coming. He could feel it. He had no desire to be outside when it happened.

But Molly was dancing by the door.

He placed the hardcover he'd been reading on the ottoman, stood up and stretched. Better to do this now than in the middle of the night. He opened the cabin door. Molly wriggled her lean, strong body past his legs. He lost her in the darkness as her black fur blended into the tree line.

"Molly, damn it," he said. "We already played this game once today."

The black mutt, more nothing than Lab, was just shy of a year and still had some puppy in her sixty pounds. By morning, she could be halfway to Grand Junction.

He grabbed his jacket from the hook by the door and his big heavy flashlight from the shelf, and stepped outside to follow her. The dog had grown on him. Four weeks ago, he'd only been back in the States for three days when he'd gone to the local animal shelter. Forty-five minutes later, Molly was sitting next to him in the truck, her head hanging out the window. An hour later, he and his new sidekick had made his first big-box-store run and had a coffee pot, an electric fry pan and an oscillating fan.

A week later, he'd moved his meager belongings to

the Donovan cabin, which sat three hundred yards down a dirt road, high in the Rocky Mountains.

It was as close to off-the-grid as one could get. The nearest town, which was being generous because it was less than five hundred people, was forty minutes away. The nearest city was twice that.

The isolation felt good after spending the past twenty years in the company of mostly men, many of whom had felt the need to talk. About their families, the jobs they'd left behind, their favorite places to eat back home. And he'd listened.

Most hadn't noticed that he hadn't reciprocated with his own stories.

He'd always assumed that once he retired after twenty years in Uncle Sam's army, there'd be a few fellow soldiers he'd want to catch up with. Share some stories about acclimating back to civilian life. Had never dreamed that he'd come home with a cloud of suspicion hanging over his head. Certainly hadn't been prepared for the hostility that he'd encountered when he'd run across men who not so long ago had called him friend.

It was a damn mess. He didn't know whom he could trust and whom he couldn't.

So he'd come to a place where he'd always felt safe. Crow Hollow. Freshman through junior years in high school, he'd spent his summers here, running between the two cabins that graced the wilderness. The McCanns' and the Donovans'. Mack McCann and Brody Donovan had been his best friends. Rich kids who hadn't seemed to understand the difference that money made.

Maybe it was only the poor kids who knew that.

It had been the happiest three years of his life. And if he'd been inclined to reminisce about his youth, it would have been those summers that he'd have remembered fondly.

But then his stepfather had gotten some crazy idea that he wanted to live on the coast and they'd packed up and moved to Oregon for his senior year of high school.

He and Mack and Brody had sworn they wouldn't lose touch. And they hadn't. Even when oceans and continents separated them over a period of many years.

What the hell would Mack and Brody think about what had gone on this past year? Even in the middle of the worst of it, he hadn't told them anything. They were active military and if they'd tried to help, it might have tainted them in some way. Ethan figured if he went down, he wasn't taking his two best friends with him.

But he hadn't gone down.

He'd survived the investigation with his career intact. But everything had been different.

And that, ultimately, had led him to this place, to chasing a stupid dog through the mountains.

"Molly," he yelled. "I swear, if you and a coyote mix it up, I'm going to root for the coyote."

His dog barked in response. He took that as a good sign. And while they'd only been buddies for a few weeks, he understood the message. *Hurry. I found something.* Last week she'd practically barked herself hoarse because he'd been too slow to acknowledge the dead raccoon that she'd stumbled over.

"I'm coming," he said. He walked the remaining fifty yards, the frost-covered grass crunching under his feet.

Molly was dancing, her nose in the air. He used his flashlight to search the ground. Nothing. He made another sweep. It was hard to see much; the whole area was thick with underbrush.

He looked higher, thinking she might have something up a tree. He ran his flashlight from side to side.

"What the hell?" he said, holding the light steady. There, barely visible through the thick branches, was a car suspended in the towering trees. The front end was badly busted up and was tilting down at forty-five degrees.

He supposed it could have been there for some time. But he didn't think so. First of all, there'd been heavy wind and rain just two nights ago, heavy enough to blow the car out of the trees. Secondly, the car still had a headlight burning. Given the noise both he and Molly had heard, he suspected it had just happened. He angled the powerful beam of his flashlight even higher to inspect the road above them. He didn't see any other cars to suggest that it had been a multivehicle accident.

Had the driver fallen asleep? Or maybe he was simply drunk? Whatever had caused him to plunge over the side of the mountain, one thing was pretty sure—if he wasn't dead, he was likely banged up pretty badly.

"Hey," he yelled. "You in the car, can you talk?"

No reply. He considered his options. He hadn't brought a cell phone with him to Crow Hollow. Reception was always spotty in the mountains and quite frankly, he wasn't interested in talking to anybody. His only good option was to hike back to the cabin, get his truck and drive into town for help.

He studied the patch of trees. They were mammoth pines, the kind with big trunks and spreading branches, crowded close together. He walked around, looking up, Molly at his heels. He stopped when he found one that had possibilities. He considered the angle of the car.

It was possible, he supposed. He'd done crazier things.

It'd be a hell of a fall if he didn't make it.

"I'm coming up," he yelled. He took off his coat, rolled his flashlight inside of it and then belted the sleeves around his waist. He was definitely going to need both hands free.

"Are you sure?" a faint voice asked.

A woman. If the wind hadn't been blowing the right direction, he probably wouldn't have heard her.

He jumped and caught the lowest branch, then pulled himself up. Found a toehold, another branch, and scrambled up another five feet. The bark was sticky and it was hell on his bare hands but he kept going. "How many in the car?"

"Just me."

He climbed faster. "Are you hurt?"

"No. Not really," she said.

He doubted that was true. A person could have all kinds of internal injuries and not realize it because of the shock of the accident. "Just hang on," he said.

For the past twenty years he'd trained every day and it was paying off now as he pulled himself up from branch to branch. Still, it was taking almost everything he had. By the time he got near the top, he was breathing hard and sweat ran down his back. He looked down. It was too dark to see the ground but he'd been keeping a rough count in his head as he'd moved from branch to branch. He had to be at least sixty feet in the air.

He untied the sleeves of his coat, unwrapped his flashlight and focused it on the car that was at a thirty-degree angle to his left, still at least fifteen feet above him. The view was impeded by branches that poked up against the car. The driver's side was toward him but from his vantage, he couldn't see her.

"Okay, I'm close," he yelled. He put his jacket back on so that he didn't have to hang on to it.

"Great," she said. He could hear her better now. He caught an edge of self-deprecating humor, as if to suggest that it was nice of him to stop by.

She'd been lucky, although he doubted she'd appreciate hearing that assessment right now. The rear axle of her car had been snagged by a thick spray of branches and that had stopped the fall. Unfortunately, the front of her car didn't have much support. One wrong move and it was going to go end over end, stopping only when it hit the ground.

"How much do you weigh?" he asked.

"One twenty-five."

Pretty slim. Hopefully pretty agile.

He studied the car and the branches holding it in place. It was hard to see where one tree ended and another started. He edged out farther, tested his weight on a branch that crossed over, found it steady enough and switched over to her tree. He shimmied in three more feet. Now he was pretty much under her car.

Together, they'd weigh more than three hundred pounds. He didn't know what the tipping point might be but he didn't want to take a chance on the branches being able to hold that much weight unless he absolutely had to. "Okay, here's what we're going to need to do," he said, purposefully keeping his voice casual. "I want you to crawl over the front seat into the backseat. Then open the door and start to work your way down. All you need to do is get ten feet and I'll have you."

There was a long pause. Finally she said, "Well, that sounds easy enough."

He smiled, appreciating the fact that she wasn't crying or screaming at him to do something. "Just keep your weight from shifting forward and you'll do fine," he said. If she didn't do it exactly right, there was a high probability that she and the car would come tumbling down, taking him with them.

He aimed his flashlight at the car. She moved and he could see her head and chest in between the headrests of the driver's and passenger's sides. He figured she was crouching on the front seat. Sure enough, a leg came over, then the second one.

The car rocked.

And he held his breath.

The tree wasn't quite ready to let go.

"How ya doing?" he asked.

"Oh, fine." He heard the tremor in her voice. She'd be crazy not to be scared.

"Open the door. Slide out, plant your feet before you grab for a branch. I'll shine my light so that you can see."

The door opened and she stuck a leg out. She had on jeans. That was good, otherwise her legs would be a mess by the time she got to the ground.

She planted her foot. She was wearing loafers, which was better than sandals but not as good as boots.

"Good job," he urged.

Next leg. She was moving slowly and she very carefully placed the second foot on the branch.

"Okay, without standing up, press down with as much of your weight as you can. See if you think the branch will hold you."

She did as instructed. The car didn't move.

"Now I want you to stand up, and try to make it one smooth motion. Don't push off on the car," he warned her, knowing that would be her tendency and that it could be disastrous. "Once you're standing, reach for a branch. Don't yank it, just lightly use it to steady yourself."

There was no response, no movement. He waited. And got nervous. "Coming?" he prompted.

"I'm going with Plan B."

Chapter Two

"Plan B?" he repeated.

"You know, that's the plan where I make some final bargains. You know, the 'hey, God, just get me out of this tree and I'll be a better person' type."

He'd made his own share of bargains over the years. As a kid, most of them had something to do with his mother keeping a job, his stepfather keeping his nose out of a bottle and him keeping his back from being blistered with a belt. So, yeah, he could understand where she was coming from.

"The wind's picking up," he said, deciding it was better not to tell her that sometimes bargain-making sucked. "I think it's time to get out of this tree."

"Okay." And she did it just perfectly. Stood up, kept her hands off the car, and reached one arm up to steady herself.

It couldn't have gone better.

Until the branch she was on cracked and she started to fall.

Ethan lunged and managed to grab her and pull her tight to his body. Then he lost his own footing and his flashlight flew. Together their weight crashed through branches and limbs. He kept one arm around the woman and groped for something to hang on to. He thought it might be hopeless until he finally managed to snag a heavy branch and stop their descent. His arm muscle strained with the effort of holding both of them until he located a branch to rest his feet on. Without losing his grip on her, he edged back toward the trunk. When he got there, he leaned back against the sticky, rough bark.

He was breathing heavily and his heart was pounding in his chest. His back had taken the brunt of the fall and he was grateful for his heavy coat. It had kept him from getting too beaten up. He had no idea how far they'd fallen but he bet it was at least thirty feet. The woman had to be scared to death.

She hadn't said a word yet. Hell, maybe she'd passed out.

He'd gotten a quick look at her when she'd stood outside the car. Slender. Not overly tall. Dark hair piled on top of her head. Now that she was in his arms, he could tell that she was at least eight inches shorter than his six-two and her shoulders and ribs were delicately female. His chin rested on her head. Her hair was silky and he caught the scent of cherries with a hint of vanilla.

As crazy as it seemed, she felt right in his arms.

Hell, maybe he'd hit his own head.

He shifted, carefully turning her in his arms. It was very dark and they were in the bowels of the tree. No moonlight filtered through.

He wanted to touch her face, to see if her features were as delicate as her body.

He kept his arms where they should be. "Are you okay?" he asked.

"I think so. Thank you," she added.

Her voice was low. Sexy. "You're welcome…" He let his voice trail off, hoping she'd fill in the blank.

"Chandler," she said.

It was an unusual name and he got a very odd feeling. "Chandler what?" he asked.

"McCann. Chandler McCann."

Ethan almost dropped her again. But he held on. Mack's little sister. She'd been a skinny little girl, with wild hair and emerald-green eyes.

Cat-Eyes.

That's what Mack had called his little sister. Ethan and Brody hadn't called her anything, never really talked to her at all. She was just their best friend's little sister. He remembered her as a quiet kid who liked her computer games.

It had been a long time since he'd seen her—not since the time they'd celebrated Mack's graduation from the Naval Academy, and Brody's graduation from college and acceptance into medical school. By that time, Ethan had already had four years in Uncle Sam's army. He'd completed flight school and had spent some time in the skies above Iraq.

He'd been about twenty-two at the time, which would have made her fourteen. She'd still been a skinny kid with braces and wild hair, but he remembered thinking that Mack's sister was going to be a pretty girl when she grew up. Brody must have thought the same thing because Ethan remembered hearing him tease Mack about having to beat the boyfriends off with a stick. Mack, who even at twenty-two was more James Bond than any of the actors who'd played the iconic hero on-screen, had calmly responded that he'd vaporize them.

While Ethan hadn't seen Chandler since then, he had

heard about her. Knew that she'd been the valedictorian of her high school class, knew that she had gone to college in Chicago on a full scholarship and knew that she'd gotten her heart broken by some jerk a couple years ago. She lived in Denver. Worked for some company that was a military contractor.

"I'm Ethan Moore." He heard her swift intake of breath and wished there was enough light that he could see her eyes. His mother had cleaned the McCann house, the Donovan house and at least twenty others. That's how he'd met Mack. That's how he'd come to spend his summers in Crow Hollow.

"Good old Walnut Street," she said. "I guess that's where we both learned to climb trees."

It was nice of her not to mention that his mom had been hired help. "I think we need to get out of this tree."

She felt him shift, just enough to look past her. She didn't know how he could see much, unless his night vision was considerably better than hers.

She wished she could have seen more of his face. Ethan Moore. He'd been one of her brother's best friends. And Mack still talked about him, spoke as though they kept in contact even though Mack's work took him everywhere.

She knew he'd be having a birthday soon. He'd turn thirty-eight next week, just two days after she turned thirty. She could still remember the year that her dad had invited Ethan over and they'd gathered around the kitchen table to share a cake. She'd been nine, he'd been seventeen.

And she'd been secretly in love with him.

And he'd pretty much ignored her every time she was in the room with him.

God, that was so long ago. Now she was here in a tree scared for her life, and her teenage crush had come to save her.

Not exactly the way she'd fantasized she'd end up in his arms.

"Here's what we're going to do," he said. "I'm going to go first. I'll guide you on where to place your feet. Branch by branch, we'll work our way down. Okay?"

She nodded. It sounded easy enough. Until she had to grab the first branch. Damn, her shoulder felt as if a ball of fire had landed there. While Ethan's body had shielded her from the brunt of the fall, her shoulder had connected with something. She gritted her teeth, determined not to complain.

He wrapped his strong hand around her right calf and she could feel his heat through her jeans. He gently tugged, guiding her to the next branch. It was slow going and by the time they reached the ground, she was clammy and terribly afraid that she might vomit after all.

There was a midsize dog with dark fur at the bottom, and it circled her.

"Don't worry about Molly," Ethan said. "She found you."

"Thank you," she said to the mutt, reaching out her good arm. The dog's fur was thick and warm and it made her realize how cold she was in her shirt, jeans and lightweight denim jacket.

Molly evidently got excited with the attention and jumped up. Both paws hit Chandler squarely on her bad shoulder with enough force to send pain skyrocketing through her arm. "No," she cried weakly.

"Molly." Ethan's voice cut through the quiet night.

Chandler managed to turn the other direction before she bent at the waist and vomited.

When she was done, she realized that Ethan was standing right next to her, his hand on her back. She straightened and wiped the back of her hand across her mouth. "I'm sorry," she said. "I hurt my shoulder and Molly caught it just right."

He didn't say anything for a minute. When he did, his voice was calm. "Okay. We need to get you inside as quickly as we can."

She could hear the sound of a zipper. Then felt something warm around her shoulders.

"I can't take your coat," she said. "I have one."

"You have a jacket," he said. "It doesn't even look as if it's lined. Now put your good arm through," he instructed. "Keep your other arm tucked at your side."

She did as he told her and in the dark, with just a little moonlight to guide their actions, he gently bundled her up. She felt warm and safe, and the coat had a comforting smell of musk and man.

"I feel bad about taking your coat," she said. It was cold and all Ethan had on was a long-sleeved shirt.

"It's fine," he said, dismissing her concerns. "Does Mack know you're here?"

"No. I didn't want to bother him. I got a text from him a couple weeks ago that he was going out of the country for the next few months. Working." Saving the world. That's what Mack did.

"So your dad knows that you're here?"

She hesitated before deciding to tell the truth. "No, not exactly."

"You're not in any trouble, are you?" he asked, perhaps reading into the hesitation.

Chandler knew she was definitely in trouble. Someone had run her off the road. But it was possible that she'd been in the wrong place at the wrong time. She certainly couldn't go around making crazy accusations against her stepmother. Not until she had more proof.

"You mean other than my car being in a tree?" she asked, forcing a light note into her voice.

"Yeah," he said.

"Not that I know of."

"Okay, good. I guess what I really want to know," he said, "is how the hell your car ended up in the tree."

She wanted to spew out the whole terrible story. But there was no way. If she told him that she'd been purposefully run off the road and that someone had circled back to verify that she was dead, any reasonable person would expect that she'd be clamoring to get the police involved. She wasn't ready to do that. Certainly wasn't ready to say "someone tried to kill me."

She wasn't ready to face that herself. Much less tell Ethan.

"I must have been going too fast. It's been a long time since I've driven these roads. I lost control, hit the side of the mountain and the next thing I knew, I was headed over the side."

"Scary," he said, his voice soft.

He had no idea. She remembered the headlights in her rearview mirror and the impact of the car against her back bumper, and shivered. "Yes. I think I flipped over in the air because my backpack and purse got thrown somewhere else in the car. I landed right side up, fortunately. The air bag inflated. I was just taking stock of my situation when you came along."

"We're lucky Molly can be a pain in the butt, otherwise I wouldn't have found you. If you can't walk back to the cabin, I can always carry you."

The idea of being in Ethan Moore's arms made her warm up suddenly. "It's my shoulder, not my legs. I can walk."

"I know that. But injuries have a way of sneaking up on a person."

"I'll be fine once I can get to the cabin," she said.

"Here's the deal. There's electricity but no heat or hot water at your cabin," he said. "I was actually going to stay there until I discovered that. That's when I moved to the Donovan cabin. Fortunately, Mack, Brody and I always had keys to both. I think it was your brother's idea. Always have a plan and a backup plan."

That sounded like Mack. And the situation at the cabin sounded rather grim. But she'd come this far, she wasn't stopping now. "I'd still like to go there. I...I need to see it." For days her world had been in turmoil. The cabin had always been there, solid, safe, comfortable. Everything she needed right now.

"As the crow flies, we're about a mile from there. If you need to stop at any point, just tell me. Don't hide anything," he said. "Knowing about someone's abilities or inabilities is sometimes the difference between life and death. All right?"

"Got it."

"Okay. Give me a minute to find the flashlight."

She stood perfectly still, afraid to move. She could barely see her hand in front of her face but somehow he was confidently moving around in the dark.

It took him less than a couple minutes to locate the flashlight. "Here we go," he said. "It was practically buried in these pine needles."

Suddenly a swath of light split the dark night and she immediately felt better.

He turned and led the way on the narrow path that required them to go single file. The terrain was rough and without her one arm for balance, she felt awkward and slow. But he never said anything. And he never got more than a couple steps in front of her before slowing down so that she could catch up.

When they reached the cabin, he stopped and turned. "Why don't you stay here for a minute and let me take a look first. All kinds of things can happen in an unattended space."

Yikes. She hadn't considered that. Just her luck, a bear had taken up residence. "If you think it's necessary," she said.

He let out a loud sigh. "Mack would kick my butt if I did anything different."

As she recalled, from all the wrestling matches that had occurred in their basement, Mack and Ethan had been very evenly matched. She reached into her jeans pocket and pulled out a small key ring with two keys. "It's this one."

"Shouldn't take me more than thirty seconds," he said.

"Okay. Be careful," she added.

He walked away. "Don't worry."

Worrying was all she'd done since she'd realized what had happened and was still happening.

She hadn't said goodbye to her stepmother, hadn't been able to face the woman who sat behind the big desk in her five-hundred-dollar suits.

While she couldn't be 100 percent sure, she was pretty confident the trail led right to that shiny desk with its silver pens placed just so.

If only Claudia Linder was *just* the CEO of Linder Automation. But six months ago, under a full moon, in the presence of twenty slightly drunk guests, Chandler and Mack being two of them, Claudia Linder had married Baker McCann, becoming Claudia Linder McCann, Chandler and Mack's stepmother.

Her dad had been over the moon about finding a second love. He'd been alone since his wife had died more than twenty years earlier.

It would destroy him if what Chandler suspected was true.

But how many would pay if Chandler turned her back and said nothing?

It had been thirty seconds since Ethan had entered the cabin and he still hadn't called for her. In fact, she couldn't hear *anything* from inside. Her heart was pumping in her chest. She wished the dog had stayed with her.

Something was wrong.

Chapter Three

The front door of the cabin swung open. A light had been turned on. Ethan stood in the doorway, his arm raised, motioning her in. She ran toward him, not caring that it jarred her shoulder.

"It's okay," he said, stepping aside quickly.

She nodded and for the first time in many days, when she stepped over the threshold into the familiar space, thought that he might be right.

She took a deep breath and the sense of family filled her lungs. The main living area of the cabin was one big room, with a kitchen on one side and family room on the other. Off to the left, down a short hallway, were two small bedrooms and a bath. The floors were all narrow slats of pine, and the round-log walls were the best that Colorado had to offer.

It had been in her family for generations. She knew the Donovan cabin was the mirror image. Her great-grandfather had built them both in the 1930s. In the 1960s, Grandpa McCann had inherited the cabins and paid for electricity lines to be strung from the main highway and had dug a well. By the 1990s, they'd been passed down to her dad, who saw no need for two cabins. Baker

McCann had sold one to his best friend, Brody Donovan's dad.

And her family had kept the other one, spending summers here since she was a child. Both Baker and Mr. Donovan had worked from home. Baker as a computer analyst, Mr. Donovan as a novelist. That flexibility allowed them to come in June and stay until Labor Day. The McCanns had stayed home the summer Sally McCann had died. Baker had barely left the basement and had stopped tinkering with the old helicopter that he was rebuilding. He certainly wasn't up to vacationing with his two children. Mack had been angry that they'd missed a summer in the mountains. Chandler had been too young to care as much. But by the next year, her dad had pulled himself together and things had gotten back to normal. Except the new normal had included Ethan Moore.

He and Mack had shared a bedroom, she'd had the other and her dad had slept on the pullout sofa. Every morning, the boys had met Brody Donovan at the end of the lane and they didn't come home until dark. They'd fished, hiked and swam in the lake. And at night, when Mack and Ethan had returned to the cabin, they'd played cards. It was how she'd learned to play poker, first watching, then finally, when she got the hang of it, they'd let her sit in on a few games.

"How are you feeling?" Ethan asked, interrupting her memories.

Every muscle ached and the pain in her shoulder hadn't gotten any better. "I'm okay," she lied.

He reached toward her, his palm open, and with the pad of his thumb, gently brushed the bridge of her nose, then her cheeks. "You've got some marks here from the air bag," he said. "Do they hurt?"

"Not really." Her cheeks were too cold to feel much else.

"We should assess for other injuries," Ethan said.

Speaking of assessing… Wow. Ethan had grown up and into his body. At twenty-two, he'd been tall and lanky. At thirty-eight, he was still lean but his frame was thicker with muscle. His hair was still buzzed short, military-style. His face had the same strong chin, high cheekbones and dark eyes.

He had a long, fresh scratch that started at his ear and ran down the side of his neck. She wondered if there were more scratches and cuts on his back from rescuing her from the tree. "I don't think I'm the only one hurting," she said.

He shook his head. "I'm fine. Nothing a little hydrogen peroxide and ibuprofen can't handle. I'm going to walk over to the other cabin and get my truck. There's an emergency room about forty miles away where we can get your shoulder looked at."

She shook her head. "It will be fine," she said. "I think I just sprained it. I don't need a doctor."

"Can I at least take a look at it? I don't have any formal training but I've spent the past twenty years with medics attached to my unit. I've picked up a thing or two along the way."

"Okay."

He unzipped the coat that practically hung to her knees. Very gently, he helped her pull one arm out and then he lifted the material away.

He gently probed her shoulder area and her collarbone. When he tried to gently rotate her shoulder, it moved but it hurt a lot. "What do you think?" she asked.

"I think you should go to the doctor. But beyond that, I'm pretty confident that you didn't dislocate the shoulder. It appears more likely that it's a soft-tissue injury, more of a sprain. We should get some ice on it." He walked over to the refrigerator and opened the freezer door. It was empty. "I have ice in my cabin," he said.

She nodded.

"We need to call the police," he said. "The accident should be reported."

"I'll do it in the morning. I want to get some sleep first."

"I suppose it's not going to make a difference." He studied her. "Are you going to call Mack?"

She might have to. But not yet. If she was wrong and the attack had been totally random, she didn't want to plant seeds of doubt. He hadn't been crazy about her father and stepmother's marriage, either. Had said more than once that there was something about Claudia Linder that he didn't like. "I don't think there's much he can do about a car in the trees."

"He'd want to help. But if he's working out of the country, it might take him a few days to get back, regardless of how much he wanted to."

"I guess." Tomorrow, in the daylight, somebody was bound to see her car. If she didn't report it, somebody else would. The car was registered in her name. It would probably only be hours before the police notified her dad and stepmother that she'd been in an accident and was missing.

Her dad would be terrified. Her stepmother was the wild card. Would she be grieving alongside her new husband or would she start to hunt in earnest?

By morning Chandler was going to need a plan. Right

now, it simply seemed beyond her. She was tired from the drive, sore from tumbling over the mountain and almost falling out of a tree, and rather discombobulated by suddenly seeing Ethan again after all these years.

Ethan reached down to pat Molly's head. The dog was crowding up against his leg, probably eagerly anticipating the next adventure.

"Like I said before, I'm not sure this is the best place for you." Ethan looked around the room.

She followed his gaze. The furniture was covered with dusty sheets. There were cobwebs in the corners and hanging over the stone fireplace. Nobody had been at the cabin for more than six months and it showed. She knew the beds would be stripped of their linens and the refrigerator would be bare.

It was cold. She desperately wanted a hot shower, but that wasn't going to happen. Still, she could probably make do. They always kept clean sheets and blankets in a tote in the closet and she wouldn't starve to death overnight. The lights were a plus. "It's not great," she agreed, "but I don't have a lot of choices right now."

"You can stay with me. There are two bedrooms, just like here," he added quickly.

"I know," she said. "I didn't think it was an invitation to…" She stopped, embarrassed. Of course it wasn't that. For all she knew, Ethan was married with two kids. She sneaked a quick look at his fingers.

No ring.

He noticed. "To hook up?" he said, finishing her sentence. "You're Mack's little sister. I value all my appendages."

She smiled, appreciating the fact that he was trying to make light of the situation. *Ethan Moore asked me to stay over.* If she was fourteen, she'd have written it in bold in her diary, with little hearts around it.

But she didn't want to drag Ethan into her mess. "I'll be fine here," she said, hoping she was right.

"You don't have any food."

"I did. I had a box of crackers and a jar of peanut butter in my backpack."

"I'll fix you a bacon, egg and cheese on toast."

She tilted her head. "That's my favorite sandwich."

He winked at her. "It's the only thing I remember you eating in the mornings. You had one every day for the entire summer, with a glass of chocolate milk."

She'd always assumed she was invisible to her brother's friends. "Do you have milk?" she asked.

He nodded. "White milk and chocolate syrup."

She smiled. "That's how I always make it."

"And I've got ice for your shoulder," he reminded her.

Even though she knew staying with Ethan may be a bad idea, she really didn't want to be alone. "You've got a deal. Thank you," she added. "I'll try not to be any trouble."

ETHAN LED THE way to the Donovan cabin, with Chandler following close. They didn't talk. He figured she was hurting and he was trying to process the past half hour.

Chandler McCann had certainly grown into a beautiful woman. When she'd entered the cabin and he'd seen her in full light, he'd been practically speechless. Her skin was lovely and it had made him crazy that she'd been marred by the chemical burns of the air bag. Those marks would heal but it was hard to see perfection harmed. Her dark hair had been piled up on her head but the strands that had escaped fell past her shoulders and were silky and shiny.

And then there were her eyes. A vivid emerald-green, with a slight tilt up at the corners. Thick, dark lashes.

She was stunning. And absolutely off-limits. They both might be adults and in any other circumstance he'd consider it, but she was Chandler McCann. Neither Baker nor Mack had ever delivered one of those "stay away from Chandler, you big lug" kind of conversations. Probably hadn't figured they needed to.

Both of those men—men he admired greatly—doted on this woman. Nobody would be good enough for her. Certainly not Ethan Moore.

The McCanns were old money in Denver. The kind that had a beautiful house in the wealthy district and cabins in the mountains. The kind where wealth was passed down generation to generation. No money had passed down when his mother had died. In fact, there hadn't been enough in his mother's bank account to bury her. Ethan had made sure the funeral was nice, though, using some of his savings. He hadn't expected anything different. He'd been sending money to her every month, knowing that her health limited the number of houses she could clean, knowing that her idiot of a husband did a poor job of providing for them. About the only thing he did well was run his mouth and swing his fist.

Ethan had survived the verbal and physical abuse his stepfather had dished out because he knew that Mack McCann and Brody Donovan were going to grow into men that others would be proud of.

And Ethan wasn't going to get left behind.

A week after graduation, he'd enlisted in the army. He'd always known he was going to have to find a different path than his best friends because there weren't any prestigious military academies or fancy colleges in his future. But he had been determined to be a man others would respect.

Which led him to the second reason why there was no way, no how, that there would be any "hooking up" between him and Chandler. Nobody would respect a man who got involved with somebody when his personal and professional lives had fallen apart. *Under investigation.*

Ugly words that had come on the heels of ugly accusations. And even though the wildebeest was finally off his back, there were still many who didn't believe in his innocence.

And that had hurt him more than he expected it would. When he'd made the decision to retire, his supporters had urged him to reconsider. *This will blow over,* they'd said. But it hadn't. And all the long months while he waited for his paperwork to be processed, he'd dreamed about a few weeks at the cabin, knowing that if there was anywhere that he could get his head back on straight, it was here.

The timing was fortunate in that he'd been here to offer Chandler a helping hand. The McCanns had been family when he'd needed it the most. Now was his chance to pay back some of that kindness.

And one didn't pay back kindness by jumping into bed with the only daughter.

He needed to focus on offering assistance and getting her back on her merry way. But something didn't seem quite right. It was almost as if the explanation of her accident had been too easy. She hadn't seemed embarrassed about her carelessness or even angry. She'd reported the facts calmly with relatively little emotion.

Which made him question whether she was telling the truth.

He rounded the last curve in the path and raised the beam of his flashlight to show the Donovan cabin. Then he turned to look at her. "Still doing okay?"

"Yes. As we were walking, I kept thinking of all the times you, Mack and Brody used to sneak out at night and meet one another. This path was well traveled. You could probably still walk it with your eyes closed."

"Almost," he admitted.

"Remember the time I tried to follow you? I got about halfway down the path and it was so dark that I tripped on something. That's when you heard me."

It had been toward the end of his last summer here and he and the others had taken a liking to fishing in the lake in the middle of the night.

"Mack tried to send me back. You said I could come but only if I wore a life jacket in the boat."

He smiled at her. "If Baker found out, I sure as hell didn't want to have to tell him that we'd taken you out on a lake, in the middle of the night, without a life jacket."

"The three of you didn't wear them. As I recall, when Mack and Brody got done fishing, they jumped over the side and swam for a while. You stayed in the boat with me."

"We were too stupid to wear life jackets," he said. "You were the smart one."

"I always appreciated that you stuck up for me. And it was such a cool night, almost magical. I could understand why the three of you were willing to give up sleep to do it."

Magical. That was a good description of most of his experiences at the cabin.

He stepped up onto the front porch, unlocked the door and pushed it open. He flipped on a light and pointed her toward a chair. "Have a seat," he said as he turned up the heat on the thermostat. He pulled a plastic bag out of one of the drawers and stuffed it with ice from the freezer. "Here," he said, handing it to her. "I've got some pain relievers, too." He walked toward the bathroom and came back with a small bottle of ibuprofen in his hand. He poured a glass of water and shook out two tablets. "Here."

"You should take some, too," she said. "Your back has to hurt from crashing through those tree limbs."

It did, but there weren't that many tablets left in the bottle. He'd save them for Chandler. "I'm fine."

She sat down in the big rocking chair that he always used, holding the ice on her sore shoulder. She nodded at the book on the footstool. "You read Mr. Donovan, too?"

He nodded. Larry Donovan, Brody's dad, had been a quiet man who stood a foot shorter than his son. He'd never heard the man raise his voice. Yet he wrote the most hair-raising, nail-biting suspense that Ethan had ever read. "Every book. He scares the hell out of me sometimes."

"Me, too. I was afraid to even look at a chain saw after I read his last one."

Molly crowded up next to her, just the way she always did to him. The dog whined and Chandler took the ice off so that she could reach out and pet her. She looked around the small cabin and smiled. "It looks just like I remember."

He nodded. "Your great-grandfather knew something about building. Both cabins have really stood the test of time. They'll be here a hundred years from now and probably look the same."

She leaned back in her chair. "I'm grateful that you were here, that you were able to help me. Are you home on leave?"

He could tell her the truth, that he was on permanent leave because he wasn't sure anyone trusted him anymore. Was sure that he'd lost *his* ability to trust. But he didn't want to have that conversation. "I retired. Had my twenty years in."

That made it seem simple. Reasonable.

She widened her pretty green eyes. "Really? So what's next for you?"

"I'm not sure. My plans were to hang out here for a few weeks and then make some decisions."

"Good for you," she said. "Maybe you'll go back to school?"

"Maybe." There was no need to tell her that he'd acquired both a bachelor's and a master's degree online while in the service. With honors.

"Or look for work?" she continued on. "With your experience, you should be fine. I'm sure there's a good job out there for you."

Was that a note of wistfulness that he detected? Was her own job in danger? But that couldn't be right. He thought he recalled Mack telling him that Baker had married Chandler's boss. "How's your work going?"

"Oh, fine," she said quickly. "You know," she added, waving her delicate hand, "if it was supposed to be fun, they'd call it play."

He smiled. "I guess. You've been there quite a while, haven't you?"

"Six years."

"The company is a government contractor?"

"How did you know that?"

He shrugged, not wanting to admit that he always listened closely when Mack talked about Chandler. Maybe it was because he'd never had a little sister of his own. "I think Mack might have mentioned it."

"We're a vendor for the Department of Defense."

"What do you do there?"

"I'm a computer analyst."

"You followed in your dad's footsteps," he said, smiling.

"I guess. Computers have always just been easy for me."

"I bet you're good at it."

She shrugged and then winced when it evidently hurt her shoulder.

"You want some more ice?" He hated that she was hurting.

"No." She stood up. "But I am really tired. If you don't mind, I think I'll just go to bed."

His mind conjured up all kinds of images it had no business doing. "I promised you a bacon, egg and cheese sandwich," he said, grasping for the mundane. "And chocolate milk."

CHANDLER SHOOK HER HEAD. It sounded wonderful, but she hadn't been kidding when she'd said she was tired. She hadn't slept more than a couple hours over the past several days. "I'll have it in the morning." She walked over to the kitchen sink and dumped out her ice bag. "How do you think they'll get my car out of the trees?" she asked, hoping her inquiry sounded casual.

"I imagine they'll have to bring in a crane. It will take somebody who knows what they're doing."

Would it attract a crowd? Would the people who'd run her off the road have stuck around to make sure that she was really dead? What would they do once it was discovered that the car was empty?

Would they start looking around the area? How long would it take them to find her cabin? Ethan's cabin?

She had to be gone by then. She couldn't put Ethan in any danger.

"You don't happen to have an internet connection, do you?" she asked.

He shook his head. "What do you need?"

One more look. Just one more chance to try to figure out if her imagination had been working overtime, like when she read Larry Donovan's books. She didn't think so. That's what had sent her out of the office in a hurry just a few short hours ago.

She wanted to try to remote into her desktop. Not that she expected to be able to. If what she suspected was true, her computer privileges had already been revoked, all permissions associated with her username shut down.

Not having access would be a little more proof.

But then what would she do with it?

Confront her stepmother?

Tell her father?

Call the police?

She realized that Ethan was waiting for an answer. "Nothing important," she said. "Well, good night."

"We'll have to put sheets on the bed in the spare bedroom."

"Just a blanket is fine."

He ignored her and proceeded to pull a shallow plastic

container out of the closet. He took the lid off and then gathered up a bottom sheet, top sheet and a pillowcase. Then he pulled out a blanket.

She helped him put the bedding on the mattress— at least as much as her injured shoulder would allow— and she was struck by the easy familiarity between the two of them. It was as if they'd been making beds together for years.

"Thank you," she said. She locked eyes with him and was pulled in by the intensity of his gaze. "I know how lucky I am that you were here tonight. I appreciate it, I really do."

He stared at her and she felt her skin grow warm. The bedroom was small, dimly lit by just a bedside lamp.

"Ethan?" she said. Did he feel it, too?

He hesitated. "Just make sure you let Mack know that I was helpful," he said, his tone light. He turned away. "Good night, Chandler."

ETHAN NORMALLY ENJOYED a beer around five o'clock, especially if it had been a particularly warm afternoon. And maybe with dinner, in the right surroundings, he'd have a glass of wine. He rarely drank late at night, though. But, he rationalized as he stood in the small kitchen, popping the top of a pale ale, the prospect of sleeping ten feet away from Chandler McCann would be enough to make a teetotaler reach for the whiskey bottle.

Why the hell couldn't Mack's little sister have grown up ugly? Or at least plain.

No. She was gorgeous and had a nice personality to boot.

She'd demonstrated tremendous composure when she'd been eighty feet in the air. Most men he'd known wouldn't have been as brave. And her shoulder had to be hurting, but she wasn't complaining.

She could have easily died tonight. That made the beer in his stomach roll and he set the bottle down.

He lay down on the couch and waited for Molly to jump up, to stretch out, to take up way more space than she should have. But she didn't move away from her spot outside the door of Chandler's bedroom. She rested her head on her paws.

He closed his own eyes, strangely content that both he and Molly were watching over Chandler.

He didn't wake up until a blast, loud and sharp, had him literally jumping off the couch. For a second, he thought he was back in the military, flying at night, and that his bird had been hit.

He got his head back in the present moment, went to the door, opened it and looked outside. The snow that had threatened all day had started to fall. There were already several inches on the ground. But when he looked up, he could still see the smoke. He judged the distance and whirled when he heard a noise behind him.

Chandler stood in the hallway. Her dark hair floated around her shoulders and the T-shirt that he'd given her hit her mid-thigh. Molly stood next to her, her nose in the air, her body on full alert.

"What was that?" Chandler asked, her voice rusty with sleep.

He stared at her. There wasn't any easy way to say it. "I could be wrong, but I think your cabin just blew up," he said. He ran his fingers through his short hair. This was all his fault. He'd known there were people who held grudges. He'd read the anonymous letters.

Had one of them snapped?

He was supposed to be staying at the McCann cabin. His mail was still getting delivered there. A reasonable person would have assumed he was there.

She still hadn't said a word. He couldn't blame her. If he was right, she'd just lost something that had been in her family for generations. She would hate him when she learned the truth.

She slowly walked toward the door and looked past him. Smoke was continuing to billow up into the sky. Molly crowded in next to them but the dog, finally showing some sense, stayed inside the cabin.

Finally Chandler turned to him. Her eyes were dark with pain. "I think I'm in trouble. Real trouble."

Chapter Four

He closed the door. "What the hell are you talking about?"

"I know you asked me earlier if I was in trouble. And I said no. I lied, okay? And we can talk that to death once we're out of here. But now, we have to go. Once the fire spreads, the road out will get blocked."

He shook his head. "I hope not. This snow will help. Plus, we've had rain all week, leaving the ground pretty much saturated. We may get lucky."

Please, please let him be right. If the fire spread, not only would it make escape more difficult, but the Donovans would lose their cabin, too. One more senseless loss. It made her sick to think that her family's cabin was gone. They had spent so many good years there. Mack would be really upset when he heard.

Of course, he'd have been a lot more upset if she or Ethan had been inside when it happened.

"I hope you're right," she said. "But even if it doesn't spread, it's going to get some attention. I know there aren't any other cabins near here but I think that blast could have been heard for miles."

"No doubt." He looked at her expectantly.

He wasn't going to be happy until he had every last

detail. Great. Maybe it would start to make sense if she verbalized the thoughts buzzing in her brain.

"What would cause that kind of explosion?" she asked.

"I'm not an expert on that," he said. "But if I had to guess, I'd say it's one of two things. Somebody may have launched a small device into the cabin and it exploded upon impact. Or, maybe somebody placed a bomb at the site, set on a timer."

Had the people who had run her off the road known the location of the McCann cabin? Neither it nor the Donovan cabin could be seen from the road.

Her stepmother had never been there but she'd certainly heard about it. Maybe had put two and two together and come up with four.

Had Ethan's invitation to spend the night at the Donovan cabin screwed up Claudia Linder McCann's math?

It would have been a safe bet to assume that Chandler was headed toward the cabin. It wasn't beyond the realm of possibility that her stepmother had somehow managed to get a bomb planted at the cabin in advance of Chandler's arrival. This was a woman who had turned a small at-home business into a multimillion-dollar operation. She was smart. She got things done.

Had someone planted the bomb and been headed back to the interstate when they'd happened to pass her on the road? Had they improvised? Figured that the mountain road presented an opportunity that they couldn't ignore?

They wouldn't necessarily have gone back to remove the bomb. That would have been a big risk if somebody had heard the accident and come to investigate. They'd probably just kept driving.

Or had they?

Ethan's other idea of how the fire might have started scared her to the point that she could hardly form a coherent sentence. A bomb launched from somewhere? That had to mean that the bad guys were somewhere close, perhaps watching the area. If she and Ethan tried to escape, would they see them and realize that they hadn't killed Chandler?

It made her want to hide under her bedcovers. But that was even more dangerous because the explosion had probably already been reported. Responders would be on their way. She couldn't wait around for somebody to realize that nobody had been inside that cabin.

"I promise that I will tell you everything I know," she said. "But, please, can we just get away from here first?"

He stared at her, his dark brown eyes intense. Then he gave her one short nod.

She ran for the bedroom to get dressed.

"Grab your sheets and blankets," he yelled after her. "No need to advertise that we were here."

That was smart. She pulled her jeans back on. She tucked in Ethan's long T-shirt, which kept the still-damp denim away from her skin. Then she pulled on her shirt.

After yanking the sheets off the bed that she'd made just hours before and hastily folding them and the blanket, she went back out to the living area and saw that Ethan had already pulled out the tote and put his bedding inside. She dropped her armful in and started to push it back into the closet.

"Leave the sheets on the floor. Keep the blankets in the tote," he said. "It's supposed to get really cold tonight. We may need them."

"Okay."

He walked into the small bathroom and she could

hear him opening and closing drawers. Within a minute, he was back in the living area carrying a small duffel bag and a backpack, both slung over the same shoulder. He had the towel that she'd used when she'd showered wrapped around his neck.

It was crazy but it made her warm to think that the same towel had been pressed up against her naked body just hours earlier.

He set the duffel bag down, unzipped it and pulled out a dark sweatshirt. Along with it came a banking envelope that appeared to be stuffed with cash.

"Wow. What did you do? Rob a bank?" she teased.

Without looking at her, he grabbed the fat envelope and stuffed it back inside the duffel. Then held out the sweatshirt. "It's cold outside. You better put this on underneath your jacket."

He clearly didn't intend to explain the money. No problem. She had plenty of other things to worry about. She slipped the sweatshirt over her head and rolled up the too-long sleeves. "Thank you."

Ethan picked up Larry Donovan's book. He walked over to the bookshelf, where there were at least forty other books. He squatted down and seemed to study the titles for just a minute. Then, very quickly, he pulled two books out and put them upside down at the end of the first row. Then four more upside down at the end of the second row. Two more upside down at the end of the lowest row.

"What are you doing?" she asked.

He just shook his head before grabbing an empty box from under the kitchen table and very efficiently emptying out everything that was in his cupboards and refrigerator. It wasn't much but she saw the eggs and bacon and regretted that she'd turned down the sandwich earlier. It had been many hours since she'd eaten.

He carried the box and set it next to the door. Then he went to the closet. After pulling out his jacket and putting it on, he reached inside again and came out with a bag of dog food. He added that to the box. Then he reached for the top shelf and pulled down two guns and several boxes of bullets. He put the ammunition in the box, next to the ketchup and mustard.

She wasn't surprised to see the weapons. Her dad had always kept guns in their cabin. It was an isolated area full of wildlife. Baker McCann had believed in being prepared.

She didn't know if Larry Donovan kept the guns in the cabin or if Ethan had brought them there. She didn't care. She was just thankful.

"Should we make sure they're loaded?" she asked.

"They are," he said with confidence. Again, he put his backpack and duffel over one shoulder and swung the rifle strap over the other. He gripped the handgun, keeping the short barrel pointed at the floor. "How's the shoulder?" he asked.

"It's fine. But maybe I'll take a few more pain relievers. Just in case," she added.

"Right." He waited until she'd gotten a glass of water and taken her pills. Then he nodded his head toward the box. "Can you handle the tote and that box?"

She suspected that he wanted to keep his hands free to deal with whatever waited for them outside the cabin. She was grateful that he seemed to be firing on all cylinders because her mind was still whirling with the knowledge that she'd be dead right now if she'd been in her cabin as she'd planned.

"Absolutely." She set the box on top of the tote and picked them both up. Then she went to stand by the door, immediately joined by Molly. She could feel the animal's excitement, as if she somehow knew the situation had changed.

Ethan came and stood next to her, carrying the large flashlight that they'd used before. On a hook next to the door was a red lanyard. He removed it, attached it to the ring at the end of the flashlight and then hung it around her neck. In the process, the back of his knuckles brushed against her collarbone.

She sucked in a breath of air. Those same hands had guided helicopters in military combat zones, no doubt with razor-sharp precision and confidence. Now they simply felt warm and full of life and she desperately wanted to grab one and cling on.

It was a good thing that her hands were already full.

A quick glance around the room told her that they'd done a good job of erasing any sign that the cabin had recently been inhabited.

She shifted the box to one hip, freeing up a hand to reach for the door. He stopped her with a shake of his head.

"Turn the light off before you open the door. Don't turn on the flashlight until we reach the truck. Stay close to the cabin and we should be okay."

The knowledge that he was also worried someone might be close terrified her, but she swallowed hard, determined to stay calm. Her wailing in fear wouldn't help anything.

He went out the door first. The snow was coming down hard, practically sideways. It would be very difficult for anyone to see them, even if they were close.

That knowledge helped her to keep moving, one foot in front of the other. The air smelled of smoke but there was no visible fire, making Chandler think that Ethan had probably been right and the fire hadn't spread.

He hugged the side of the cabin and she sensed, rather than saw, his progress. She stayed behind him and practically ran into the truck before she saw it. He opened the passenger-side door. "Get in," he whispered.

She slid onto the seat, pushing several folded newspapers out of the way, and almost yelped when Molly jumped in and over her, taking the middle of the seat.

"I'll take those now," he said, reaching for the tote and the box. She handed them over and heard a scrape behind her as he put the items in the back of the open truck bed. When he got in the driver's side, she realized that he'd put his duffel bag and backpack in the back, too. And the rifle. He'd kept the handgun and the ammunition and he placed both of them under his seat.

"Doing okay?" he asked.

Hell, no.

"I'm good," she said. "Will your things be okay in the back? Nothing will fly out?"

"Not at the speed we'll be traveling. It'll be okay once we're on the highway, too. I strapped everything down." He started the truck and she heard him unzip his jacket. Then the towel that he'd had around his neck, which was still mostly dry because he'd protected it from the snow, was in her lap. "Dry off," he said. "Then you may want to use it on Molly. Otherwise, every time she shakes, it's going to be another shower for the both of us."

"I'm going to be forever grateful to Molly," she said, rubbing her face dry. "She found me. Are these newspapers for her?"

"No." He flipped on his windshield wipers and cleared the windshield of snow. That's when Chandler realized that the weather must have started with freezing rain or sleet because there was a thin layer of ice on Ethan's windshield. He turned on the defrost. "I realize that it's rather old-fashioned, but I still like to read a newspaper."

"Me, too. My dad always read the newspaper. Front to back."

"I know. Ready?"

She nodded.

"Good. Let's get the hell out of Dodge," he said. "I'm not going to use my lights. Can you shine the flashlight on the road? It should be enough for me to see a couple feet ahead but won't be as visible from a distance as truck lights."

Chandler couldn't imagine that they were going to attempt to navigate icy, snow-covered winding roads with only the aid of a flashlight. They were dangerous on dry days in broad daylight—much less in a bad winter storm in the middle of the night. But she kept her mouth shut. She pulled the strap of the flashlight over her head, gripped it in her hand, leaned forward with one arm braced on the dash and lit the way.

It was barely a dent in the darkness, but evidently enough for Ethan.

When they passed the road that would have led them to the McCann cabin, she turned in her seat, wishing that she could have a closer look. "I wonder how bad it is." Her father was going to be so sad about the loss.

"I'll come back and check," Ethan offered. "But first I'm going to get you out of here."

She put her hand on his arm. "You can't come back. It's too dangerous."

"Nobody will even know I was here."

"I thought you flew helicopters. Not that you were some super-duper spy."

He turned his head. "Super-duper? Not hardly."

He was selling himself short. She didn't know much about his military career, but she remembered overhearing Mack and her dad talking about Ethan and that he was frequently in the middle of heavy combat situations.

"If you're going to circle back, I'm coming, too."

He didn't respond.

"Ethan," she prompted.

"I don't think that's a good idea."

"I have to," she said simply. "I have to see it with my own eyes."

She heard him sigh. "Okay. But for now, we're both getting the hell out of here. There's going to be a lot of activity and I don't want somebody to stumble over us by chance."

When they came to a fork in the road, she expected him to go right. Instead he turned left.

"Where are you going? The highway is that direction."

"This is the back way out. Emergency vehicles will come in on the other road and I don't want to meet up with any of them. This road isn't as good but the truck will handle it. I'm counting on the fact that most people don't even know it's here."

She hadn't known about the road but then again, it had been years since she'd been at the cabin. Hopefully whoever was after her didn't know about it, either.

He was right about the quality of the road, which

was really more of a path, with big ruts and snow-filled holes. Her car would have never made it. It was work just to keep the flashlight steady, and with each dip and sway, Molly's wet body slid on the seat, crowding close to either her or Ethan.

They crept along at fifteen miles an hour for another mile or so. She knew it was the fastest Ethan could go without much light on a road that was almost washed out in places.

"I never knew you drove a truck," she said. It was mindless chatter but she couldn't stand the silence broken only by the *swish-swish* of the windshield wipers.

"Just bought it four weeks ago when I got back to the States. I may never drive a car again."

"A pickup truck and a dog. You're sort of a country song."

He turned his head and she switched the flashlight from the road to his face for just a second. He was smiling. "All I need is a cheatin' wife."

She didn't think he'd ever married. Every once in a while, over the years, she'd make a casual inquiry of Mack about the marital status of his two best friends. Brody had come close but his fiancée had left him practically standing at the altar. Ethan, it seemed, had been married to the military and had hardly come home much after his mother died many years ago. She remembered Mack mentioning that Ethan was such a talented helicopter pilot that the army was quick to take him up on his offers to defer his leaves and remain available for flying.

"No cheatin' wife for you," she said, verifying her suspicions.

"Cheatin' or otherwise," he agreed.

How nice.

Too bad they had to meet again after all these years under these circumstances.

After what seemed like forever, they finally reached the highway. The back end of the truck slid back and forth as tires grabbed for pavement. There had to be several inches of snow already on the ground. Ethan flipped on his headlights. She could see a fire truck approaching, its lights flashing and its siren blaring. Not far behind it were two SUV-type emergency vehicles with lights blazing.

Once they were safely past them, she said, "We should stop soon if we're going back."

"It might be best if we keep going," Ethan suggested.

He was probably right. But she didn't want to leave Crow Hollow without seeing the damage firsthand. And he'd been confident that he could get back undetected. "I need to go back."

He didn't argue. "There's a house up here on the next hill," he said. "It sits back a good half mile off the road. I'll pull into the lane."

She waited as Ethan slowed before coming to a stop on the highway. He killed his lights and then backed the truck into the dark lane. He pulled in a hundred yards and turned off the engine.

She felt invisible and it was a great relief. She heard him shift in his seat and knew that he was waiting for the explanation she'd promised.

"I lied earlier when I said that carelessness caused me to have the accident."

"Okay."

"A car bumped into me. Three times. On the third time, it was hard enough to send me flying. I sort of bounced off the mountain wall and went skidding off the side."

He didn't say anything for a minute. When he spoke, his voice was hard. "Do you know who was driving this car?"

"No. I think it's possible that it was a vehicle that passed me, coming from the other direction. Then it turned around to follow me. If it was, then I think it was some kind of SUV, one of the bigger ones. I wasn't paying that much attention when I first saw it. I think there were two people in it."

"So the vehicle hitting you was definitely deliberate?"

"Oh, yeah. A few minutes after the accident, someone was up on the road. I'm sure it was the people from the vehicle that hit me. I could only hear one of them clearly. It was a man. He was convinced I was dead and he was happy about it."

"I don't understand. Why would anyone want to hurt you, Chandler?"

She sighed. "It might be helpful if I give you some background. Almost everyone at my work has either secret or top secret security clearance. The work we do for the Defense Department is pretty specialized."

"What exactly do you make?"

She hesitated. Old habits were hard to break. Maybe easier for some. It was beginning to look that way. But she still felt bound to the confidentiality agreement that she'd signed.

"Let's just say that we specialize in stealth technology."

"Now who's the super-duper spy?"

She shook her head, knowing that he couldn't see her.

"I'm the computer geek. Unfortunately, sometimes the computer people see more than they should."

"And you saw something that has people wanting to force cars off the road, to blow things up?"

"That's what I'm not sure about. It all happened so fast. A couple nights ago, we upgraded several of our computer servers. One of the servers hosts our email system. I was troubleshooting a problem and in the process, looked at some emails that had come in to various people in the company."

He didn't respond.

"I have top secret security clearance," she explained. "But still, I know that information is always shared on a need-to-know basis. So I tried to pick emails that seemed very innocent. I clicked on one titled Strawberry Short-cake Recipe." She paused. "I like desserts."

"And…"

"And it was set up like a recipe, with ingredients and cooking instructions. But the quantities looked odd. I'm sort of a math geek in addition to being a computer geek. So I started looking at it closer."

"What was it?"

"It was written in code. There were a couple pieces that I wasn't able to figure out. But I think it was a confirmation of delivery."

"For?"

"That's what I'm not sure of. But…"

"But what?"

She hesitated. "I'm fairly confident it was confirmation of a delivery of raw materials and product specifications for one of our most advanced systems."

He whistled softly. "Someone in your company is

selling secrets to the enemy. And the means to reproduce technology that could be used against Americans."

"I think so," she said, her voice soft.

"Who was the email addressed to?"

"That's the problem. It was addressed to somebody who no longer works for the company. An administrative assistant. Her in-box should have been deleted but the Help Desk must have missed that. But it doesn't make sense that this person sold the data. She would never have had the security clearance necessary to see this information in the first place."

"Did you know this person well?"

"Not well. She had worked for Claudia. She left the organization without much notice a few months ago. I didn't know of any way to reach this woman, plus I didn't necessarily think it would be a smart thing to do. I tried to search the sender but all I ran into was a dead end."

"What did you do then?"

"I started digging."

"Understandable," he said simply.

"Our system, like most computer systems, electronically stamps every action that is taken. Every keystroke. Every transaction. It's a clean audit trail."

"And you found something?" he asked.

"I found something that was interesting, to say the least. You see, it's only been recently, with the latest software upgrade, that we've been able to audit viewing."

"Viewing?"

"Yes. Viewing is when somebody pulls up a screen but doesn't take any action. Simply looks at the data. Just recently our system began stamping that activity and can tell us how long the person was viewing the screen."

"And you found that somebody had recently viewed the specs on this particular product?"

"Two people. One was another analyst, just like me. His name is Marcus White. The other," she said, unable to keep the misery out of her response, "my stepmother, Claudia Linder McCann. She's the CEO. She's always been the CEO. She's only been my stepmother for the past year."

She heard his soft hiss.

"Dicey," he said finally.

She laughed, glad that she still could. "It's not as if she doesn't have permission to look at data. She owns the company. She can look at any data that she wants. But she doesn't. That's not her job."

"Did you ask her about it?"

"No. But I ran a report of all the other screens that she'd recently viewed. There were twelve of them. Every screen was related to this one product."

"So then you went to your stepmother?"

"No. Maybe I should have. But you have to know Claudia Linder. There's always been something about her that made me uncomfortable. I just couldn't put my finger on it. I didn't really care when she was simply the CEO. I started to care more after my father fell head over heels in love with her."

"But you said that someone else also accessed the screens."

"True. And it's possible that Marcus would have needed to do it for his work. He's the analyst supporting a couple of the engineers who are working on this project. There's really no reason for him to be looking at the screens, but maybe he was troubleshooting a problem. I just don't know. I do know, however, that he was recently really upset at work. He applied for a promotion and didn't get it. I really thought he would go get another job somewhere else. He's very talented. But he stayed."

"Stayed with bad intent, perhaps?" Ethan offered. "Your stepmother or Marcus White. Two choices."

"Yes, I would think that Marcus would have been aware of our new ability to track viewing. Probably not Claudia. That's sort of in the weeds for a CEO. Anyway, I was trying to decide what to do when I realized that there was some hidden code. Code that I hadn't written. But somebody had, creating a program that ran in the background. I think it was basically an early warning system, designed to let somebody know that somebody else had accessed the screens. I got the heck out of the system but realized that if they were savvy enough to have set up that program, then they were likely savvy enough to track my IP address—my computer address," she added.

"I assume Marcus White would know how to set that up. Would your stepmother?"

"She could have asked another analyst to do it for her."

"Did you tell anybody?"

"No. I shut down my computer, grabbed my purse and my backpack, and was halfway back to my apartment when I decided to come here. And if I'm right about what happened tonight, I think that somebody tracked the activity back to my computer and maybe realized I'd figured out what's going on."

"Your company was designing this product for the government, right?"

"Yes."

"If you're right and this information was sold, that's treason."

The silence hung heavy in the air.

"Worth killing for," she said finally.

"I'd say so," he answered. "Your stepmother would have known about the cabin. Would Marcus White have known?"

"I'm not sure. I may have mentioned it to him. We've worked together for over five years. His parents live in Grand Junction, which is quite a ways west. Still, he probably knows the general area. Would certainly have traveled Interstate 70 between Denver and Grand Junction many times. Plus, if the Help Desk had deactivated the administrative assistant's username, which they are pretty good about doing quickly after someone leaves, Marcus would have had the capability and access to reactivate it."

"Okay. Earlier you said that you grabbed your purse and your backpack. You didn't get out of the car with them."

"I know. They're still in the car. I probably should have tried to grab them when I exited through the backseat but I was too scared that a wrong movement would tip the car."

"You did exactly right," he said. "You got out safely. That's always the first priority."

She turned to him. "What's going to happen when the authorities find my purse and other things in the car and I'm not there?"

THE FIRST THING they would do, Ethan figured, was track her name and car registration back to her house. "Do you live alone?" he asked.

"Yes."

He felt an absurd sense of relief.

"Well, the cops will probably talk to a couple of your neighbors. Do they know your father?"

"Some of them do. After he retired, he used to come over and cut my grass for me. The woman next door was always inviting him in for lemonade."

"Well, then, I suspect it won't take long for the news of your accident to get to your dad."

He heard her quick catch of breath and knew that her first instinct would be to call her father, to make sure that he didn't worry about her. "Call your dad. Tell him what's going on."

She shook her head. "I wasn't happy about my father's wedding. Dad and Claudia had had a whirlwind relationship. And I was worried that Dad was moving too fast. I did try to be happy for him but I don't think I hid my concerns all that well."

It had been difficult getting used to the idea that Claudia, the CEO that rarely interacted with the employees of Linder Automation, was now her stepmother.

And unfortunately, the more she got to know her, the less Chandler had liked her.

"My dad and I had a big argument shortly after he and Claudia got married. He was upset because I didn't attend an awards ceremony where Claudia was getting an award. I tried to tell him that she never invited me but she'd told him something different. I guess he believed her."

"So you can't go to him with accusations that your stepmother is committing treason and tried to run you off the road unless you're sure of it."

"Exactly. I just hate that he'll be worried. Me missing

and the cabin blown up. None of it will make any sense. He's going to call Mack and it will drive Mack crazy, especially if he's out of the country working."

If he knew anything about his best friend, Mack would plow through hell or high water to get back to the States.

He'd protect his sister with his life.

And he'd expect Ethan to do the same.

Chapter Five

"This is a mess," she said.

It was hard to argue that. But it wasn't necessarily *her* mess, and that was weighing on Ethan's conscience. Maybe the explosion at the McCann cabin had nothing to do with Chandler and what she'd stumbled upon at work.

Maybe it was because of him.

But to explain that, he'd have to explain the whole crazy situation. And how safe would she feel with him if she suspected that even a portion of the charges the military had brought against him were true?

How would she feel if she suspected that he'd sold out his buddies, causing eight to die?

Might be enough to send her running off into the night. Without protection. Without a fully loaded gun and someone who knew how to use it.

So he kept his mouth shut. And told himself that he was doing it for her. Certainly not because he was afraid of what he'd see in her pretty green eyes if she knew the truth.

"You're sure it's safe to go back?" she asked.

He regretted telling her that. But he was confident that they could go back in on foot which would allow them to approach quietly, from an unexpected direction.

They could cut across the fields and it wouldn't be much more than a mile.

He wasn't concerned about finding his way, even in the snow. He, Mack and Brody had walked this area every summer day for years. A few fences may have been put up since he was a teen but he doubted there was anything that he couldn't navigate around, even in the dark.

But even a mile could be a long way in several inches of snow. It was going to be a wet, slippery, difficult walk. He had on boots but she had just her loafers. And she had an injured shoulder. But he didn't think there was a chance in hell that she was going to let him go in alone. And he wanted to see it. Wanted to know whether he'd been the target. Wasn't exactly sure what he was looking for that would confirm or deny that but he wanted a look.

"We can get there," he said. "Here's what I think is going to happen. The emergency response folks are going to make sure that the fire is out. They're going to light that area up and while your car is some distance from the cabin, I think it's possible that somebody will see your car. If that happens, some brave soul is going to get a ladder and very carefully climb up, in an effort to assess the status of the people in the car."

"And when there's nobody inside?"

"I imagine that they'll search the immediate area. When they don't find anything, at daybreak, a massive search will ensue. The first assumption will be that a body or bodies were thrown from the car. They're going to think that they're working against the clock, that someone who is injured and caught up in a tree or lying on the cold ground is living on borrowed time."

She was quiet for a minute. "As bad as things are, I'm feeling pretty lucky right now."

"You're right. You got out of the car and neither of us was in the cabin. We both got lucky."

"Do you believe in luck running out?" she asked, her tone soft.

"I believe that luck favors the prepared."

"That's good enough for me."

"The people who did this probably aren't going to be satisfied until they know for sure their mission is accomplished. They're going to want to be close enough to know that a body was recovered. That may work to our advantage."

"We'll be watching for them and they won't necessarily be watching for us," she said.

"Right. But it may not be easy to pick out the bad guys. While the cabins are pretty isolated, it was a big blast. Some locals may come to see what's going on."

She wiped the palms of her hands on her blue jeans. "Nothing is ever easy. Let's go." She opened her door.

He took an extra minute to grab the gun and ammunition that he'd shoved under his seat. When he had first gotten back to the States, he'd had a quick layover in Oregon. Had visited his mother's grave and gone to the storage locker where he still kept some things, including the handgun, which he'd purchased many years earlier. He'd told himself that he was headed toward the mountains, and everyone carried a gun there. But he'd also felt better knowing that he was armed, in the event that some fool really believed that he could possibly have sold out his friends, his country, and came after him.

When he'd realized that Larry Donovan kept a fully loaded shotgun at the cabin, too, he'd felt even better.

And he'd brought it along for extra insurance. But for right now, the Glock felt just right in his pocket.

He got out of the truck and walked around the front of it. Chandler had gotten out and was standing next to her door. He shone the flashlight on her. It was snowing hard and her dark hair was catching the fresh flakes. Under any other circumstances, it would have made a beautiful picture.

"Let me get one more thing," he said, reaching into the box in the back of the truck and pulling out the binoculars that he'd tossed in at the last minute.

They weren't military quality, but would certainly be better than nothing. He strung the lanyard over his neck. He started to shove the lid back on the box and stopped. He grabbed his duffel where he'd thrown his extra jeans, shirts and underwear. He pulled out a pair of thick white socks. "Your shoes are going to get soaked and your feet are going to get cold. Not much we can do about that. I'll take these so at least you'll have a dry pair to put on later."

The minute he said it, he knew he'd screwed up. Her pretty green eyes filled with tears.

"What? I'm sorry. You don't have to wear them." He stumbled over his words. Chandler had been a rock up to now, taking everything that had come her way. And he'd made her cry with socks.

She put her hand on his arm and he held perfectly still, not wanting to lose the connection.

"Thank you," she whispered. "For getting me out of the tree. For taking me to the Donovan cabin. For getting me away from the fire. For caring that my feet are going to be wet and cold. I'm grateful, Ethan."

She leaned across the foot that separated them and

kissed him. Her lips were soft and warm and he desperately wanted to pull her into his body, to have her
wrapped around him.

But he forced himself to just stand still, and when
the kiss ended and she pulled back, he was proud that
he didn't beg her not to stop.

She didn't say anything.

He wasn't sure his throat would work.

After a long moment of uncomfortable silence, he
pulled his hood up and started walking.

FOR THE MOST PART, she kept up pretty well. There was no
conversation as they walked, him leading, her following
close behind. She figured he was concentrating, trying
to make sure that he had his bearings. She simply focused on putting one foot in front of the other. She was
bordering on exhaustion and her shoulder hurt like hell.

But even that couldn't keep her from thinking about
what it had felt like to kiss Ethan Moore.

It had been impulsive and a little awkward. At the
same time, it had felt completely right.

Not that he'd seemed to feel the same way.

Maybe he'd been embarrassed. It was hard to say.
Certainly, he hadn't seemed inclined to discuss it, and
that hadn't changed over their mile walk.

He'd been right about the emergency crews. There
were flashing lights and voices calling out to one another, their language indiscernible, their presence on the
normally quiet mountain horribly intrusive.

While she didn't know the terrain nearly as well as
he did, she wasn't surprised when she realized that they
were approaching the property from the rear, where a

bluff butted up to the McCann property. It was the most logical vantage point.

That worried her some, because what if someone else had the same perspective and with each step, they were closer to stumbling over the creeps who had pushed her off the road and most likely firebombed the cabin? It was almost enough to make her run the other direction. But she didn't. She had Ethan next to her and he made her feel safe.

When they were still a little ways away, he held up his hand, stopping her. "Close enough to see. Far enough away not to be seen," he said quietly.

"Is it safe?" she whispered back.

"The only way up onto this bluff is the way we came. You have to know the property really well to know that. It's the best place for us."

He looked through the binoculars, studied the scene for a long moment, then slipped the lanyard off his neck and handed the binoculars to her. She assessed the situation below.

The snow was so heavy that it was difficult to see. But it appeared that her family's cabin was destroyed. Whatever had caused the explosion, it had been effective. The modest structure had imploded, with side walls and ceiling collapsing upon one another. There had been a fire, that was evident, but it appeared to have been contained within the structure.

The emergency vehicles they'd seen were gathered around the perimeter. One firefighter continued to douse the structure with water coming from the tank. The others were standing around, talking to one another.

She couldn't stand to look at it one more minute. She handed the binoculars back to Ethan and closed her eyes, trying to block the horrific image. What was she going to tell her father?

She opened her eyes when she felt Ethan shift. He had the binoculars up to his eyes.

"What?" she asked.

"Activity," he said. "One of the guys just answered his cell phone and suddenly, everybody is running for their vehicles. The two smaller vehicles are leaving. If I had to guess, I'd say somebody just reported your car in the trees. I suspect they're going to leave the fire truck here to make sure the fire doesn't reignite, and the other two are going to the scene."

"Can we get to the car from here?"

She heard him sigh. "Yeah. But we can't take the path we took earlier. It's too close to the road and someone might see us. We can circle around but that means we'll have to cross the creek."

She was already pretty wet. How much worse could it be? "Let's go," she said.

"Your feet have to be cold."

"Of course. But I'm not stopping now."

"I thought that's what you were going to say."

It was another ten minutes of slipping and sliding through the snow before they got to the creek. She stopped, catching her breath, while Ethan ran the flashlight up and down the banks. The water was covered by snow. "It's usually only four or five inches deep," he said, "but with all the rain we've had this week, I'm betting the water level is higher than usual. Plus, there's probably some current that we'll have to fight."

"We should probably hang on to each other." She held out her hand.

He shook his head. "I'll carry you across."

She snorted. "Don't be ridiculous," she said.

"I'm not being ridiculous. There's no need for both of us to get wet."

She thought about that. "What about your gun? You can't carry me and it."

"I'll carry you piggyback. The way Mack used to," he added.

She remembered how her brother would let her climb onto his back. Then he'd race around the yard and she'd squeal until he dumped her off.

It might work. "What if you drop me?" she said.

"Then you'll get wet," he said nonchalantly.

He clearly wasn't planning on dropping her. "I really don't think this is necessary," she said.

"Take off your shoes," he instructed.

"Why? They're already so wet and muddy that I'll have to throw them away."

"But at least they're some protection for your feet. I don't want you to lose them in the creek and then you'll be barefoot. That's a recipe for disaster."

It was not worth arguing about. She took off her loafers and stuffed one into each of her sweatshirt pockets.

He put his gun and his flashlight down on a stump. Then he squatted, she jumped, and his very capable hands were suddenly under her upper thighs, adjusting, settling her.

It was oddly intimate, even though they were both wearing wet blue jeans.

"Okay?" he asked.

Oh, yeah. Ethan Moore asked me to stay over and within hours, I had my legs wrapped around his waist. Her entry into her teenage diary was getting better by the minute. "Ready when you are," she managed, trying to stay still. He'd been unresponsive to her kiss. A squirm here or a thrust there might send him into a catatonic state.

He picked up his gun and flashlight and they half slid their way down the bank. She heard his boots break through the ice and splash in the water.

It took just seconds to cross the narrow creek. Still, she was terribly grateful for the sweatshirt that he'd given her and glad that it had escaped getting wet. Something that wouldn't have happened if she'd tried to walk across the creek.

He bent at the knees and she slid off his back.

"What's your favorite pie?" she asked.

"Huh?"

"All the way across I kept thinking, *I owe Ethan big-time.* In those circumstances, my go-to solution has been to make a pie."

He was silent for a minute. "Cherry," he said. "Warm. With vanilla ice cream."

"I didn't say anything about ice cream."

"I know. There should always be a bigger goal."

"Vanilla is kind of boring."

"Traditional. Comforting. Dependable," he countered.

It was a silly conversation to be having. Especially in the middle of the night, on foot in the mountains, in a blinding snowstorm. And wet to boot.

And after somebody had tried twice to kill her.

No wonder it felt good to engage in the ridiculous.

"Okay. Vanilla ice cream, too," she said.

"Excellent. You know, that's what your hair smells like."

That stopped her in her tracks. "Vanilla ice cream?"

"Not just that. Like wild cherries with a little vanilla. I like it."

Ridiculous had just turned hot. He liked the way she smelled.

"Good shampoo," she said weakly.

He laughed. "Well, I didn't think it was pie filling. Let's get going."

Her face warm, she pulled her loafers out of her pockets, put them on over her wet socks and started walking.

THIS TIME THEY did not have the advantage of being able to watch from up high, a good distance away. To see anything, they had to get close.

At the scene, somebody had set up three battery-operated lights. They lit up the area fairly well although the heavy snow made it difficult to see fine detail. They didn't need that ability to see some guy dressed in a yellow rain slicker half climb, half slide down a ladder. He had a purse and a backpack slung over his shoulder.

"Car is empty," the man said.

There was a general mutter of disbelief and dismay. It would be a difficult search in the heavy woods in fresh snow.

They watched as he carried both the purse and the backpack over to a parked SUV. He reached into the purse, pulling out her billfold.

"Guess the mystery is solved," Chandler whispered.

It was only a matter of time before Baker McCann knew that his little girl was missing. And Ethan knew that by daybreak, there'd be an army of volunteers in these woods, attempting to find Chandler.

The smart thing would be for her to turn herself in now. It would save a whole lot of worry for Baker and

Mack. And save the volunteers a whole lot of trouble searching the woods unnecessarily.

"It's not too late," he said, voicing his thoughts.

"I think it might be. It was too late the minute I started looking at the records of who had viewed those screens."

"You're sure you can't tell your father about your suspicions?"

"My dad waited twenty years to remarry. He told me that he never wanted to until he met Claudia. Now I'm going to accuse her of treason? I can't do that without proof."

"But if it's true…"

"I know I have to do the right thing. And I will. I just hope I'm brave enough," she added, her voice full of doubt.

"You're brave," he said. "Hell, you climbed out of a car that was suspended eighty feet above ground."

"Maybe I should join the circus," she muttered.

Now wasn't the time or place to try to convince her. "So now what?" he asked.

"I'm going back to Denver, to Linder Automation. I've thought of a couple more ways that I can check the computer activity associated with that particular technology."

"Earlier you asked about internet access. Why go all the way back to Denver when you could drive thirty miles, get an internet connection and remote in?"

"I'm fairly confident that my username has been disabled. I won't be able to remote in. But I actually have another username. When we do upgrades, we have to run scripts to test the new software. When I'm testing, I have a different username. It makes it easy for me to audit what I've tested. I don't think they will have thought to disable my test username. But because of our intense need for data security, I never set my test username up with remote capabilities."

"How will you get into the building?" he asked. "I suspect you all have swipe cards to enter certain areas. If your computer access has been disabled, don't you think it's true that your entry access is also gone?"

"I'm sure you're right. I'll just have to figure something out when I get there."

She was walking into danger and he was pretty sure he wasn't going to be able to convince her otherwise. "Maybe wait a few days? When Mack hears that you're missing, nothing will keep him away."

"I can't. Every minute that I delay is another minute that my father is worried sick about me. Plus, the longer I wait, the more likely that somebody will cover up their tracks and I won't be able to get to the information that I need. I have to move quickly. I know it's a lot to ask, but could you take me as far as Glenwood Springs? I know that's west when I need to go east, but there I should be able to rent a car at least."

"You're going to drive back to Denver? The roads are getting bad."

"I'll be all right," she said, dismissing his concern.

Mountain passes blew shut all the time. It would be dangerous. "You can't rent a car," he said. "You'll have to show your driver's license, your credit card."

She sighed and he understood. She wasn't frustrated with him, just with her situation. "I'm kind of bad at this, aren't I?" She paused. "Okay, this is even more to ask. Would you be willing to use your credit card to rent the car for me? I promise that I'll pay you back."

"No."

He could almost feel the disappointment roll off her. "I understand. I do. This is a mess. You're smart to stay out of it. There must be a bus that goes from Glenwood Springs to Denver. I'll take that."

"You don't need a damn bus. I'll take you."

"No." Her refusal came fast. "I can't ask you to do that."

"You didn't ask. I offered."

She was silent for a long minute. There was just enough light that he could see her put the binoculars up to her eyes once again. She watched the scene for several long minutes. When her head jerked, he got nervous.

"What?" he asked.

She handed him the binoculars. An SUV had pulled up and a young woman wearing a big coat and knee-high boots was standing next to the vehicle. She was pointing to a young man who was carrying a camera and a tripod.

"Local news," he said. "It would have taken them a while to get here. Probably the biggest story they've had since the summer fires."

"This is getting worse by the minute," she said. "I have to get to Denver. Right away. Before the story becomes any bigger."

"Okay. Maybe we'll beat the worst of it."

Or maybe they were about to walk right into the worst of it.

Chapter Six

The snow intensified as they headed toward Denver and the wind started really blowing. Even though they were on an interstate, there had been very little traffic and for the past twenty minutes, they hadn't seen another car.

"It should start getting light soon," Chandler said. Not that light would necessarily help the situation. But she felt the need to say something. There had been no conversation for some time, probably because they were both exhausted.

Except for the short rest they'd gotten before the cabin exploded, they'd been up all night. At least she was warm and dry. Before walking back to the truck, she'd put on the dry socks Ethan had carried. Of course, they were wet by the time she'd climbed into the cab of the truck. Ethan had given her another pair of dry socks and aimed the heater vent at her wet jeans. Once they were on their way, she'd pawed through the box of supplies and made them both peanut butter sandwiches. They'd drunk orange juice straight from the bottle because they didn't have any cups.

She'd been grateful for the food, but after her hunger had been somewhat satisfied, it made it even harder to stay awake and several times she'd caught herself closing her eyes and drifting off for just a minute. She'd woken with a start, grateful that Ethan was able to stay alert.

He had to be just as tired, if not more. He'd had the additional stress of keeping the truck on the snow-covered road.

She felt horrible that she'd dragged him into this situation. He could still be warm in his bed, asleep.

No. Instead, he was battling with many inches of snow and a sharp wind that was creating drifts that the truck was having trouble plowing through. Several times, the back end had started sliding and she knew that it was only Ethan's superior reflexes that were keeping them on the road.

"This is worse than I expected. It's coming down so fast."

"Yeah. If I had to guess, I'd say a couple inches an hour. We'll be okay," he said, assuring her.

She wasn't so sure. The only consolation was that anyone following them was battling with the same snow and likely wasn't handling it as well as Ethan.

They drove for a couple more miles when in the distance Chandler saw flashing lights. At first she thought it might be police or fire trucks, but as they got closer, she saw it was a big snowplow.

How was there going to be enough room on the road for both of them? She held her breath as Ethan inched his big truck over. She expected the plow to keep going but it slowed and the driver waved at them to stop. He leaned out of the cab of the plow.

Ethan rolled down his window. "Hey," he said.

The driver wore overalls and had a stocking cap pulled low on his head. He was at least sixty. "Road is closed fifteen miles up ahead," he yelled. He was still difficult to hear over the wailing wind.

Chandler leaned forward in her seat. "Closed? Totally?"

"Yes, ma'am. We might have been okay if not for the wind picking up. Denver and everything two hundred miles west is socked in. I'm on my way home. They're pulling the plows off the road."

She had to get to Denver. "How long before the road is open again?" she asked.

"Depends on when it stops snowing," the man said. "Last I heard, this is supposed to keep up for most of today." He wiped his gloved hand across his mouth where ice crystals were quickly forming on his gray mustache. "Next side road to the left takes you into Wheatland. That's where I'm headed. You might want to follow me. Bessie here will blast through anything that's blocking the road." He patted the side of the noisy beast lovingly. "Not much there but at least you'll be off the road. Dot's is open 24/7 and you can probably hunker down there and ride out the storm." He raised his hand and waved. "Good luck," he yelled. He pulled his head back inside the cab of the snowplow and raised the window.

Ethan rolled up his window and looked at her. "What do you think?"

She couldn't think. She was too tired. Too worried. "What do you think Dot's is?"

Ethan shrugged. "If we're lucky, a nice little restaurant with great food and a wine list. If we're not, a gas-station-convenience-store combination with hot dogs that have been rolling around in some machine for eight hours. In either case, I'm assuming there's heat. And quite frankly, that's probably our biggest need right now."

"We've got blankets," she said.

"And they will help but we'll still need to use the heater if we are stalled on this road for any length of time. I've got less than half a tank of gas left. We'll eat through that quickly."

The smart thing to do was to follow the snowplow. But that meant going backward. Losing time. And she had this horrible feeling that time was not her friend.

But she'd be risking her life if she insisted they stay on the road during a blizzard. Risking Ethan's life. "Let's follow the snowplow."

Turning around on the snow-covered highway took just a moment and they easily caught up with the snowplow. The orange beast cleared a path for them, all the way up to the front door of Dot's Diner. It was a stand-alone building with a metal frame and a row of windows across the front.

The lights were on and Chandler could see people inside. "I'm guessing no wine list."

Ethan nodded. "Probably a meat loaf special."

"Will Molly be okay out here if we go inside?" she asked.

"For a few minutes." He reached under his seat and pulled out a leash for the dog. "I'll let her out for a minute to do her thing."

Chandler waited while the dog inspected several piles of snow before deciding which one to yellow. She peered out her window. The snow was beautiful, really. If it wasn't so frustrating.

Ethan opened the door and Molly jumped inside and promptly got snow on Chandler. She used the towel to wipe the worst of it. "Lie down," she said. "Be a good girl and I'll bring you a cheeseburger."

Molly was either agreeable or hungry for meat because she did a couple circles on the seat and then plopped down.

Chandler opened her door and trudged through the deep snow into the building. Inside, there was a worn linoleum floor, ugly green booths, an empty pie case, a Spanish-speaking radio station blaring in the kitchen and a small television in the corner that was on mute but had storm updates running across the bottom of the screen.

There was also the smell of coffee and something cinnamon.

And it was blessedly warm.

They took a seat in one of the ugly booths. There were four other diners. Two older men sitting side by side at the short counter. They both wore brown overalls and work boots. There was a pile of dark coats on the empty stool next to them. There was also a young couple, probably both early twenties, who sat in the booth farthest from the door, holding hands across the table. They had already eaten because their dirty plates were pushed to the side.

There was no sign of any employees until a woman, stick-thin, wearing white uniform pants and a white smock, came through the swinging door that separated the dining room from the kitchen. She had a cell phone up to her ear.

"You could call your dad," Ethan said quietly.

Chandler shook her head.

The woman in white put the phone down, looked in their direction and held up a pot of coffee. When they both nodded, she grabbed two empty coffee cups. As she approached the table, Chandler could hear the click of her shoes on the tile floor. Her gray hair was not quite as short as Ethan's but darn close. When she got near the table, Chandler could see her name tag. Roxy.

Chandler wasn't sure what a Roxy should look like but it wasn't this stern-faced, almost military-type presence.

"Storm blow you in?" Roxy asked.

Chandler nodded.

Roxy poured coffee with a comfortable familiarity, holding the pot high above the cups. "Where you headed to?"

Chandler opened her mouth to speak but Ethan cut her off. "Nebraska. My wife and I drove all night. We need to pick up our kids from my mom's."

Wife? Kids? Nebraska?

What the heck? It dawned on her that what she'd said earlier remained true. She was bad at this. Fortunately, Ethan was better. He'd concocted a story without blinking an eye.

"Snowplow stopped us and told us the road was closed," Ethan continued on.

The woman nodded. "Happens a couple times a year. It's blowing worse than usual. You want some breakfast?"

Chandler nodded and expected the woman to hand them menus. But she simply stood there.

Even though they'd had the peanut butter sandwiches, Chandler was still hungry. "I'll...uh...take some pancakes," she said. "And some bacon, too."

Ethan took a sip of his coffee. "I'll have the same but can you add two eggs over easy and a side of hash browns?"

The woman turned and went behind the counter and through the swinging door. Chandler took a drink of her own coffee. It was delicious. She appreciated that Ethan had dropped the idea of calling her dad. She wasn't ready to do that.

"Hope the kids have been good for Grandma," she said.

He raised an eyebrow. "It was the first thing that came to mind."

"It's fine. Better than fine. Really smart. If somebody is tracking us and happens to stop here, Roxy's not going to connect me to some too-inquisitive-for-her-own-good computer analyst."

"Exactly."

They sipped their coffee for several minutes. "Do you want children, Ethan?"

He set his coffee cup down hard and one of the men at the counter turned to look at them. Ethan gave him a little wave and the man turned back around.

"I haven't given it much thought," he said.

"You'd be a good dad."

He shrugged. "I don't know about that. My own dad died when I was ten."

She'd have been two. She might have heard somewhere along the line that Ethan's real dad had died but she'd never really given it any thought that they'd both lost a parent when they were very young. Maybe that was the basis of the connection that she'd always felt with Ethan.

She'd met Ethan's stepdad a couple times when he'd picked Ethan's mom up after she finished cleaning their house. The man had scared her for some reason. He always had an angry look on his face. "What about your stepdad?"

A look came into Ethan's eyes that she couldn't decipher. But she saw him push away his coffee, as if he'd lost the taste for it.

"What ever happened to him? I know your mom is dead, Ethan. I'm sorry about that. Dad and Mack went to the funeral, but I was out of the country at the time on vacation. I guess I never heard what happened to your stepdad."

"Two years after my mother died, he drank too much one night and ran his car into a lake. He drowned."

"I'm so sorry."

"I wasn't. It was too bad he managed to avoid the lake as long as he did." Ethan sat perfectly still for a long moment, then shook his head, as if in disgust. "Makes me sound like a coldhearted bastard, doesn't it?"

She knew that wasn't true. Ethan Moore was a good guy. The past several hours had proved that. Plus, as a young girl, she remembered her father talking about how Ethan watched out for his mother. He used to carry her heavy cleaning supplies and in the winters, when it got dark earlier, he always took the route home from school that would allow him to walk her home.

"He must have been a really bad man," she said. Without thinking, she reached out and touched his hand.

His skin was warm, warmer than hers, and she felt the heat travel up her arm. With the tips of her fingers, she rubbed the fleshy part between his index finger and thumb.

He didn't move. She wasn't sure he was even breathing.

"Ethan," she said, her voice hesitant.

He pulled his hands back, breaking the connection. Then he picked up his coffee cup and drained it.

She put her hands in her lap. They were shaking and she sure as heck didn't want him to see that.

"Look," he said, "let's just get something to eat and then we'll try to find a place where we can buy some gas. Maybe get a couple hours of shut-eye."

He looked tired. Heck, he had to be tired. He'd been awake all night, battling treacherous roads.

"Once the road is opened up, we'll take off," Ethan added.

"What if it takes all day?" Chandler asked, hating that she sounded petulant.

"I know it's hard to be patient but you heard the snow-plow driver. He said the storm has pretty much shut down Denver and everything west of it for two hundred miles. Maybe nobody makes it in to work today at your place?"

It was possible, but it ate at her that she was so close but could virtually do nothing to finish the trip. "Damn snow," she muttered. "Damn mountains."

That made Ethan smile and she felt the mood lighten. She was happy about that. She hadn't meant to stir up ugly memories or make him uncomfortable with her touch.

"I don't see how they're going to be able to get my car out of the trees," she said, determined to keep to safe topics.

"You're probably right. They already know it's empty, so that won't be their first priority. They may initiate a search-and-rescue operation but the heavy snow will hamper that effort."

"The car that hit me, that knocked me over the side of the mountain, is still out there."

Ethan nodded, looking serious. "And we have to

assume that they know that your body wasn't recovered. We have to assume that if they were responsible for the explosion at your cabin, that they also know by now that there were no bodies found inside. We have to assume that they won't stop looking."

"But will they think that I'm headed back to Denver? Maybe I'm running the other direction?"

"Maybe. But you have family and friends in Denver. Two touch points that people need when times are tough."

"Claudia Linder McCann is not a touch point."

"But is she a traitor to her country?"

"I wish I knew," Chandler said. "I just wish I knew."

They didn't speak again until Roxy returned with their food. The pancakes were big and nicely browned and the bacon was crisp, just how she liked it. She took a few bites. "We could have been stranded in a much worse place," she said.

Ethan nodded. "Yeah, this is good. I guess I didn't realize how hungry I was."

They finished up their breakfast and when Roxy presented the bill, Ethan pulled cash out of his pocket. It made Chandler realize that she had very little money on her. She normally paid for everything with her debit card, but that was in the purse that was now likely in police custody.

"Thanks for feeding me," she said after Roxy left to get Ethan's change. "Not only have I lost my credit cards, which I wouldn't be able to use anyway, I only have a couple dollars that I had in my jeans pocket."

"I've got plenty of cash."

She'd seen the wad of it. "Why so much? Were you planning on buying something for the cabin?"

He shook his head. "I…I guess I just like having cash around. Maybe because I grew up in a house where as a kid, if I had to ask my mom for ten bucks for something at school, I'd see this panic in her eyes. And when we went to the grocery store, we only had so much money. So if I wanted something that wasn't on the list, something else had to come off the list. I hated that. I swore that when I grew up, I was always going to have cash. Plenty of it. It makes me feel happy just knowing it's there." He shook his head. "That probably seems weird to you."

She smiled at him. "It makes a lot of sense. Things that happen to us as kids definitely shape our whole lives."

"Your mom died," he said, his tone gentle. "How did that shape your life?"

She appreciated that he was direct. "Well, you know she had cancer. She died when she was thirty-seven. Not really all that much older than I am now. Every year on my birthday, I can't help but think that soon, I'll have been alive longer than my mother was."

"And that bothers you?"

She shrugged. "It makes me scared sometimes. I worry that my life could be over before I get to do all the things I want to do or accomplish everything I want to accomplish. Do you ever think of things like that? After all, your dad died young, too."

He shook his head. "When you're in the military, you accept that death is a possibility. You don't want it but you accept it. I guess I just didn't worry about it."

"You're lucky."

"I guess I—"

Ethan stopped when Roxy approached the table with

his change. He took some of it but handed her a very nice tip. "That's yours," he said. "My wife and I are going to try to catch a little sleep in our truck. You don't mind if we keep it parked in your lot, do you?"

The woman shrugged. "Don't see that it much matters," she said. "Won't be all that busy today. Nobody is going out in this unless they have to. But if it's sleep you want, maybe I can help you out. There's a room with a private bath upstairs. I rent it out to a sales guy who calls on this region. He stays here during the week and goes home to Utah on the weekends. Anyway, he left yesterday when he heard the snow was coming. I got up early this morning and cleaned the room and put clean sheets and towels in there so that it would be ready when he came back next week. I'll let you folks have it for fifty bucks a night."

Ethan looked at Chandler.

A warm bed with clean sheets and a hot shower to ease the tension in her sore shoulder. It sounded like heaven. "We'll be leaving just as soon as the road opens up," Chandler said.

Roxy shrugged her narrow shoulders. "Fifty bucks, whether you stay two hours or all night. Same difference to me. Same amount of work for me to clean up after you."

"We've got a dog in our truck," Ethan said. "Good dog," he added. "Can we bring her inside with us?"

The woman shrugged. "Twenty more for the night and you clean up any mess she makes."

Ethan pulled cash out of his pocket. "Sounds like a fair offer. You're sure Dot doesn't have other plans for the room?" he asked, nodding his head at the sign that hung over the counter.

"There ain't been a Dot here since the Vietnam War ended. Her husband came back and they took off somewhere. Every owner since then has kept the name. I didn't see any reason to change it. What was I going to call it? Roxy's? Sounds like a bunch of hookers and people would take one look at me and know that I could make more money selling eggs."

There wasn't much to say to that. Chandler looked at Ethan.

"We'll take it," he said.

Roxy held out her hand for the money.

Ethan gave it to her. "You wouldn't happen to have a couple plastic containers? I'd like to have them for my dog. One for food and the other for water."

"I got all kinds of that stuff. Wait here."

She went back into the kitchen and returned in less than a minute. She tossed one empty plastic container in Ethan's direction and handed the container that she'd already filled with water to Chandler.

He was grateful the woman hadn't balked at having Molly in the room. He couldn't have left the dog alone in the truck all night—not with the freezing temperatures.

He didn't much care about having a bed to sleep in. He'd slept in much worse places over the years than a truck with nicely padded seats. But the look on Chandler's face when the woman had described the room convinced him.

He'd seen her efforts to stay awake while he'd been driving. He'd lost track of how many times she'd nodded off, only to wake up with a jerk minutes later. He'd wished she'd simply give in and sleep but she'd refused to do that. And there was no way that her shoulder wasn't hurting. She'd taken the last of the ibuprofen with her breakfast and that would help, but real rest would help more.

Roxy led them to the back of the restaurant, and opened a door to a small dark hallway. At the end was another door and stairs leading up.

"That door opens to the parking lot. I'll unlock it now so that you can get your dog."

Ethan made his way to the truck, realizing that the tracks that he and Chandler had made earlier coming into the diner were already gone, filled in by swirling snow. He opened the door and whistled softly for Molly, who leaped off the seat and promptly floundered in the snow that came up past her belly. Ethan grabbed his duffel bag and Molly's leash. "Don't embarrass me inside," he warned the dog.

He clipped the leash on Molly and led her back into the building. She was covered with snow by the time they got inside. Ethan used his hands to brush off the worst, thinking that Roxy wouldn't be too happy with Molly tracking all over everything.

But the woman barely gave the dog a glance. She led them up the stairs, into another narrow hallway that had a door on each side. She opened the door on the right.

The full-size bed took up most of the small room. There was a scratched-up dresser in the corner with a straight-backed wooden chair next to it. There was an oscillating fan in the other corner that was not plugged in.

It was intimate.

In a very minimalistic kind of way.

But it looked clean and he figured that Chandler could take the bed and there'd be just enough room for him and Molly to stretch out on the floor.

It would be fine for a few hours.

Chandler put down Molly's water dish and the dog immediately took a big drink. Then she quickly sniffed around the whole room before settling on the rug next to the bed.

"I'll get the heat going for you," Roxy said. She walked over to the thermometer on the wall and twisted the knob.

"Roxy," Ethan said, "I'm wondering if I could ask a favor. Because we're on our way to get our children, we want to leave here as soon as the road opens up. I know you've got the television going downstairs. If the status of the road changes, would you tell us? I'll throw in an extra twenty for the room."

"I'll keep an eye on the television. But I'm leaving at eight tonight. Sharp. No need to stay open all night in this weather. You're on your own until tomorrow morning if you're not gone by then. By the way, if you're going to want dinner, get your food order in by seven."

Ethan could see the panic in Chandler's eyes at the thought that they might be delayed that long.

"That's the bathroom," Roxy said, pointing at the closed door across the hallway. "Takes a minute for the hot water to get going but it'll last you a nice long time." She turned and walked to the door of the small room, then stopped and looked over her shoulder. "I imagine it's hard to be separated from your children at a time like this, but I suggest you both get some sleep. You look like you could use it."

Ethan and Chandler waited until her footsteps had faded before closing the door. Molly, who had jumped up on the chair, was looking at them expectantly.

"She's something," Chandler said.

"For a minute I thought I was back in the army and that I should salute."

Chandler sat down on the bed. The mattress appeared firm. Probably so the woman could make exact corners when she made up the bed.

"Got a quarter?" she asked.

Ethan fished around in his pocket. "No. Why?"

"Isn't that what happens in basic training? They make you bounce a quarter on your bed to make sure it's made right."

It should have surprised him that he and Chandler were thinking along the same lines. But it didn't. It felt normal. "Basic training was a thousand years ago."

Chandler waved a hand. "You say that as if you're two thousand years old."

"I'm almost thirty-eight." This past year he'd aged in dog years.

"I know how old you are, Ethan." Her pretty green eyes never wavered from his. "You're not too old and I'm old enough."

Chapter Seven

"What the hell did you mean by that?"

"I think you know what I mean," she said, sounding irritated. She waved her hand. "Never mind. I can be a little impulsive at times. This was one of those moments."

He could feel the tension in the room, and as it had been when he was a kid, he had a physical reaction. His skin got warm and his eyes seemed more sensitive to the early-morning sunlight that bounced off the snow and leaked in through the thin curtains.

He could literally feel the blood coursing through his veins. Could feel parts that had no business having any reaction to Chandler McMann start to tighten and harden.

He shifted his stance.

She boldly stared at him. He wasn't fooling anyone.

"I've known you my whole life," she said. "You were my brother's cool friend. I guess I always figured I might see you again someday, but I certainly never expected that I'd be sharing a room with you. But we are. We're both adults, Ethan. We don't need to make this bigger than what it is. But we also don't have to ignore that this could be something nice, something good, in the middle of something that quite frankly isn't very nice or good."

She made it sound so easy, so damn reasonable. They'd hook up and have a couple hours of fun and when this was all over, go on their merry ways.

Under normal circumstances, he might accept the offer on the table. She was gorgeous. They were both unattached. They had a few hours to kill.

But it didn't matter that her suggestion made his body tight with almost uncontrollable need. Chandler McCann was the daughter of the man he respected most in this world, the sister of his best friend. And he was a man with nothing. No job, no real place to live. He wasn't what she deserved. "I think you better get some sleep, Chandler. We've got a long day ahead of us."

She blinked her eyes fast and he realized that she was fighting back tears.

"Don't you dare cry," he said. That would be his undoing. "I'm doing this for you. I'm doing this because it's the right thing to do."

"Whatever." She stood quickly. "I'm going to take a shower." Then she left the room without looking back.

CHANDLER WENT INTO the small but clean bathroom. There was a shower stall but no bathtub. She turned on the water and quickly realized Roxy had been right. It took forever for the water to heat up.

She put the toilet seat down, sat and let the tears come. And come and come. All the frustration of the past few days, all of the fear and desperation of running for her life, all the angst and embarrassment of the past few minutes, it was a watershed moment. And when the water finally got hot and she stepped into the small stall, she was still crying.

Was she destined to always make a fool of herself around Ethan? She could still clearly remember the year she was fourteen and they'd been celebrating Mack's and Brody's college graduations. She'd gotten up one morning and Ethan had been in the kitchen, wearing nothing but pajama bottoms that rode low on his hips. He'd had his back to her, making scrambled eggs. He'd turned to her, smiled and asked if she'd wanted some breakfast.

She'd been determined to impress him, to make him notice her. So she'd lied. Had told him some wild story about how she wasn't sure she could eat because she'd been with friends the night before and they'd gotten someone older to buy them alcohol.

She'd thought he would think it was cool, that maybe he'd see her in a different light. He'd see her as old enough to be interesting.

But he hadn't acted as if he thought it was cool. He'd lectured her that she was too young to even be thinking about drinking. He'd been so serious, so damn grown-up about it. And she'd wanted to be mad at him. But then he'd said, "You're too nice a girl to have something bad happen to you. Promise me that you won't do that again."

And she'd known that deep down, Ethan Moore cared about her. Maybe even liked her. It had been overwhelming. She'd mumbled something about a promise and then she'd run for the shower because she simply had to get away. Had to get control of the emotions and feelings that were flooding her hormone-cursed teenage body.

When she'd finally come back to the kitchen, he'd been gone. She'd moped around the house for days until her father had finally demanded she tell him what was wrong. When she'd refused, he'd said that he assumed that she felt bad about the drinking, proving that Ethan had mentioned it to her father. She'd been so angry that she'd blurted the truth out. *I never had a drink. I just wanted Ethan to think that I was cool.*

Her dad had nodded and said that he understood but he'd gotten that same look in his eyes that he'd gotten the day she'd told him that she'd started her period.

She hadn't seen Ethan for all these years but evidently nothing had changed. He still wasn't interested.

By the end of her fifteen-minute shower, the tears had finally stopped. She stepped out onto the tile floor, being careful not to slip. It felt wonderful to be clean. When she rotated her shoulder gently, it felt pretty good.

Taking the end of her towel, she wiped the steam off the mirror that hung above the sink and leaned close. Roxy was right. She looked tired.

Maybe that was why Ethan had turned her down flat.

If it were only that easy. A little sleep could fix everything. The next time she offered, he'd jump on it.

She didn't think so. It hadn't been a *boy, I'd really like to but no, thanks*. It had been a *hell, no*.

Was it because he couldn't ever see her as anything but Mack McCann's little sister who ate egg sandwiches and drank chocolate milk? Was it because he resented that she'd pulled him into a situation that was getting worse by the minute?

Was it because she just didn't do it for him?

That one was really tough to take.

She pulled a hair dryer off its hook and punched the on button with more force than necessary. Then she did her best without a comb, finger-drying her long hair.

When she finished, it wasn't perfect but at least it was clean and dry.

She picked up her dirty clothes, which were nice and toasty from the heat that was pouring out of the tall radiator. She pulled her bra and panties from the pile. Maybe she couldn't wash everything but at least she could have clean underwear.

She used a little of the hand soap and warm water to clean the delicate fabric. After rinsing her lingerie, she hung it over the radiator to dry. She picked up her shoes and also put them on the radiator.

She wrapped the towel around her and tucked it in to keep it secure. Then she once again crossed the hall and opened the bedroom door.

Ethan was stretched out on the floor, his eyes closed, his breathing deep. He was still fully dressed.

Chandler stared at him. He was such a handsome man. So very male with his broad chest and his slim hips.

And he'd said no. She should respect that.

She climbed into bed, still wearing her towel, and closed her eyes.

ETHAN DIDN'T OPEN his eyes until he was sure that Chandler was asleep. Then he sat up, careful to stay quiet.

She had the covers pulled up with one bare arm on the outside, and he could see the edge of her towel peeking out above the covers. She had such lovely skin, so pale, with just a few freckles. Her dark hair floated around her face, spreading across the white pillowcases.

He was a damn fool. She'd offered and he'd turned her down. He hadn't had much of a choice. He sure as hell wasn't going to disappoint Baker McCann or Mack by taking advantage of the situation.

What they both needed was a little perspective. And a little sleep. It was almost eight, the time when most reasonable people were just starting their day. There'd been nothing reasonable about the past ten hours. From the minute he'd crashed through the tree boughs only to realize that he had Chandler McCann in his arms, he'd been solely focused on keeping her safe.

At the time, he'd thought his biggest worry was going to be her sore shoulder.

An explosion in the middle of the night had quickly upped the ante, and now a damn race across the mountains in the middle of a blizzard was bordering on sheer madness.

Was it possible that her stepmother was selling military secrets? Could Baker McCann have given his heart to a monster?

No, not the Baker he knew and respected and loved. Yes, *loved*. He'd been a young boy in need of a father figure, and Baker had been more than just an acceptable stand-in. He'd inspired Ethan, given him hope.

He wasn't going to sleep with the man's daughter.

He recalled what Roxy had said about the shower— that the hot water would last a long time. He hoped the same was true about the cold.

He carefully got up, grabbed his duffel bag and left the room. When he opened the door, Molly lifted her head but made no move to follow him.

When he opened the bathroom door and saw Chandler's underwear drying on the radiator, he almost forgot his resolve. She might have a towel on but she didn't have anything on underneath it.

She'd said she was "old enough." Her lacy dark blue underwear screamed "sexy and old enough." And that was a hell of a combination.

He turned on the cold water and ducked his head under.

After his shower, he shaved and brushed his teeth and got dressed in clean clothes. He stuffed his dirty ones into his duffel bag and crossed the narrow hallway.

Chandler was still fast asleep, although she'd turned over in the bed. She'd thrown off the covers and her towel had come undone.

He could see most of her back. Soft skin. Delicate ridge of her spine. Gentle rise of her buttock.

Hell. He closed his eyes, turned and lay down on the floor, facing away from the bed.

He needed to get her to Denver, help her find a safe way back into her old company and then leave her in Baker's or Mack's safe custody.

CHANDLER WASN'T SURE how long she'd slept, but when she woke up, she could see Ethan asleep on the floor. She quietly stretched, making almost no noise, but still his eyes immediately flipped open.

She grabbed the edges of her towel, holding them together. She didn't want him to think that she'd gotten so crazy that she was literally going to throw her naked body at him.

"Hi," she said, determined to get back to where they'd been before she'd propositioned him.

He smiled. "Sleep well?"

"Yeah. What time is it?"

He looked at his watch. "Almost lunchtime. We slept for about four hours. Are you hungry?"

"I could probably eat. I'd like something to drink for sure."

"I'm going to take Molly outside while you get dressed. Then we can go downstairs, grab some lunch and check on the weather conditions. I'm assuming the road is still closed or Roxy would have been knocking on the door."

"Maybe she got busy and couldn't get away?" she said, hoping for the best.

He shrugged, then shifted from his back to his feet in one smooth motion. It was that same agility that probably had allowed him to climb the tree.

He'd likely be a very graceful lover.

That thought made the heat flood to her face.

"Are you okay? Does your shoulder hurt?"

"A little," she said, willing to let him think that was the reason she looked a little hot and bothered. "Once I get up and going, it will be fine."

He nodded, opened the door and whistled for Molly. The dog immediately started dancing around and Ethan clipped on her leash.

"You don't happen to have a comb I could borrow, do you?" Chandler asked, pulling at her long dark hair.

He reached into his duffel. "Here," he said, tossing it at her. "I've got my toothbrush and some toothpaste, and I'm okay sharing it."

She ran her tongue across her teeth. It would be wonderful to brush them. "Thank you."

He grabbed the items from his bag and tossed them in her direction, as well. They landed on the bedspread. "I'll be back in just a minute," he said before he left.

She climbed from the bed, wrapped the towel tight

and walked to the bathroom. Her underwear was dry and she pulled it on. Then her jeans and her shirt.

She slipped on the socks Ethan had lent her and her loafers, which were dry but beat up from the walk in the snow.

She looked in the mirror. The burn across her nose and cheeks was fading. She ran Ethan's comb through one section of her hair. Then another, until it was ready to be gathered up and secured with the clip. Then she brushed her teeth.

When she returned to the room, Ethan and Molly were already back and he'd made the bed. He was sitting on the end of it.

"That was fast," she said.

"Molly's not a big fan of the snow."

But she did seem to like her food. Ethan had dumped some of the dry dog food into the empty plastic container. There was still plenty of water in the other one.

She handed him his toiletries. "Thanks. I've never used anyone else's toothbrush before."

"Not your boyfriend's?" he asked. "Christivo, right?" he added, surprising her.

"How did you know his name?"

"Mack might have mentioned it," he said casually.

She'd met Christivo Kappas the first semester of her senior year in college. Professor Christivo Kappas. She'd needed a liberal arts credit and philosophy sounded as good as any.

She really should have picked a theology class.

He spoke of concepts and teachings that she'd never heard of, and she'd thought he was brilliant. She'd approached him after class one day with a question, and that had led to coffee, which led to quiet dinners in his small apartment. By the fifth week of class, she'd been sleeping with him. It had been a fantasy-like romance, with him pursuing her relentlessly. The experience had been quite heady, really. She'd agreed to keep the relationship a secret, believing that he was concerned about how his boss might interpret his having a relationship with a student.

He'd been her first lover and by the end of the semester, she'd begun planning her wedding. She'd told Mack and her dad about the relationship and they'd been insistent about meeting Christivo. But he'd had one reason after another as to why he wasn't able to.

Six weeks into the second semester, he'd dumped her, admitting that he was married and that his wife and two children lived three hours away, in their hometown.

She'd been so embarrassed that she hadn't told her family the truth. She'd lied and said they'd mutually agreed to part.

"Christivo might have shared a toothbrush with his wife but he never shared one with me," she said, unsure why she wanted to share that bit of information with Ethan.

He frowned. "His wife?"

"Yeah. Mack doesn't know that, however, and I'd appreciate it if you wouldn't tell him. Even though it's been eight years, he'd probably still want to kill him for me."

"Maybe I'll do it for him," Ethan said, his voice hard.

She shrugged. "It was a long time ago."

He stared at her. "But there's been no one else?"

"I've dated," she said, feeling the need to defend herself. "Quite a bit," she added.

"But never got serious with anyone again?"

She hadn't been that brave. "I was busy. Working

full-time, and I just finished getting my master's degree last year."

He nodded but she could tell that he didn't believe her.

What else could she say? *I was waiting for you or at least the image of you I've carried around in my head since I was fourteen.* He'd be scared that she'd left crazy germs on his toothbrush.

There were two different men sitting at the counter when they got downstairs. These guys were a bit older but dressed almost identically to the ones who had occupied the stools that morning. Whoever sold the brown overalls in town had a real monopoly going.

There was a husband and wife and a noisy baby in a high chair. The only other occupied booth had one lone man drinking coffee and eating a piece of chocolate cream pie.

Which Chandler took one look at and promptly decided that she was having a piece.

They took the booth farthest from the door. Ethan took the side facing the door; Chandler had her back to it.

When Roxy approached the table, she smiled at them. "Looks as if you got some sleep. You don't look quite so hollow-eyed."

"The bed was really comfortable," Chandler said. "Wasn't it, honey?" she added, looking at Ethan.

"Felt good to stretch out," he replied, not missing a beat.

She wanted to roll her eyes but she didn't. When Roxy pointed at a chalkboard on the wall, Chandler quickly read through the six choices. Ethan had been right about the meat loaf special. "I'll have the meat loaf. And a piece of that pie," she added, inclining her head in the direction of the lone diner.

"I'll take the egg salad sandwich and the beef barley soup," Ethan said.

"You going to let your wife eat her pie alone?" Roxy asked.

Ethan shook his head. "Nope. I'll take a piece of that, too."

As Roxy walked away, they switched their attention to the television. The volume was low but they were close enough that they could hear the announcer. "Worst storm in ten years." "Snow falling at more than two inches an hour." "Interstate 70 expected to be closed for at least another twelve hours."

That meant it would be at least midnight before they could get on their way. And that was the most optimistic perspective.

"I need a book," Chandler said.

"Huh?"

"I'm going to go crazy without anything to do for twelve more hours. I need a book or a magazine or something."

"I got a deck of cards in the truck," he said.

Sometimes when Mack, Ethan and Brody had played cards in their basement, her dad would make the boys a snack and she got to take it down to them. One time, when she was probably eight, she had begged and begged to be included in the game. Mack had given her a few chips and said she could play until she lost her money. Then he'd given her a crash course in poker.

She'd promptly lost most of her chips until suddenly she started winning. It had been so much fun.

Then Mack had realized that Ethan was throwing in

good hands so that she'd keep her head above water. He'd yelled at Ethan, who hadn't bothered to defend himself.

It was just one of the many reasons she'd fallen in love with him.

As she'd gotten older, the boys would sometimes let her play. Mack would always tell Ethan, *Now, don't let her win.* And she wasn't sure if he did or not because she'd become a pretty good poker player.

"Cards might work," she said. "Do you still play poker?"

He nodded.

Roxy approached the table with their food. The meat loaf came with mashed potatoes and gravy and corn. It looked delicious.

They ate in silence, although not really because the television droned on and the baby was banging his spoon on the metal high chair tray.

While they were eating, a woman entered. She was tall and had a stocking cap pulled on low over her long brown hair. "Oh, my God, Roxy, am I ever glad you're still open. Isn't this the worst storm ever?"

"She's not making me feel better," Chandler whispered.

"Just enjoy your meat loaf. Live in the moment."

"Thank you, Master Zen."

He smiled.

The woman sat on one of the empty stools. "I'll have to take mine to go," she said. "Horace is out helping the county keep the roads to the hospital open. But he said he'd be back by three to take me home. Give me some soup and whatever you got that's chocolate for dessert."

A woman after her own heart. Chandler pushed her meat loaf aside. She'd eaten most of it. It was time for pie.

She ate it all and had her hands resting on her full belly when Roxy came back with the check. Again, Ethan pulled out cash, leaving Roxy a great tip.

"Roxy, is there anyplace we could buy some ibuprofen? I've got a sore knee," Ethan said.

"Fantail Drugs. Jaylene there at the counter runs the place. It's just down the road. They carry about everything. The kitchen is just packing up her food. You can follow her back."

"I'll go upstairs and get our coats," Chandler said, grateful for the chance to get some fresh air. Heck, maybe they sold women's underwear and she could pick up a couple extra pairs. And Ethan could give up sharing his toothbrush.

She slid out of the booth. "I'll be back in a minute."

Chapter Eight

Chandler wasn't back when the door opened and two men came in. Ethan pretended to be solely interested in eating his pie. They both had dark hair and pale skin. One was short, probably not over five-three. His chin looked as if he'd had a run-in with a dull ax blade. The other was taller, maybe around five-ten. Hard to guess their weight because they wore big coats. They had snow on their pants up to their knees.

They looked at everyone in the small diner, glancing quickly past the family with the baby and the two men at the counter. They settled on Jaylene at the counter, who had her back to them.

They shared a quick moment of eye contact and then separated, coming at her from both sides. She glanced at one, frowned, then at the other. There was no sign of recognition in her round eyes.

The two men shared another quick glance and Ethan could see the frustration in their eyes. They'd been interested in Jaylene until they'd seen her face.

From the back, they'd have noticed a lone woman with brown hair down to the middle of her back.

Of course, it was curly and a dull brown. Certainly not a silky, shiny dark brown that smelled like tart cherries and vanilla. But these guys had probably been given the shorthand version.

Ethan was sure of it. They were looking for Chandler. He wanted to beat the hell out of them.

But he forced himself to stay in his seat.

He'd always been a good fighter, had learned to protect himself, and later, when he'd had to protect his mother, had handled a man who had outweighed him by fifty pounds.

But they probably were armed and someone might get hurt. What if a stray shot hit the child? What if they had reinforcements out in the car who managed to somehow grab Chandler when Ethan's attention was on these two?

He wouldn't take the chance. Not unless he had to.

"Can I help you?" Roxy asked, sounding a bit annoyed. She didn't know these men, that was clear. And she didn't like how they'd come up and surrounded Jaylene.

"Two coffees to go," the short one said. "Heavy on the cream. And a couple pieces of whatever you've got for dessert."

Roxy made fast work out of pouring the coffee and putting lids on the cups. Then she put two pieces of the chocolate pie into a container with two plastic forks.

Hurry up and leave, he willed. Chandler would be back any minute.

Roxy took the white plastic sack to the counter. The men handed her a bill and waited while she counted out the change. The tall one asked her something but Ethan couldn't hear because the baby was still clanging his spoon. Ethan saw Roxy shake her head and shrug. Then she handed them the bag and walked away.

They left, letting in a blast of cold air.

Ethan shifted in his seat, enough that he could see the street. Sure enough, within a minute, a big black Suburban rolled past with the two men inside, keeping in the path that the snowplow must have cut sometime when he and Chandler were sleeping. The vehicle handled that portion of the road fine, but Ethan figured they would have trouble if they got somewhere that hadn't yet been plowed.

Ethan felt stupid. He'd been the one who had told Chandler that they had to assume that the men would keep looking. But when the storm had continued and the road conditions had worsened, he'd gotten complacent. He really hadn't figured that somebody would be hot on their trail.

These people seemed to want to find Chandler in the worst way. And he didn't think it was so they could tell her that they were worried sick that she was missing.

Roxy bagged up Jaylene's order next and the woman pushed a few dollars across the counter, not waiting to get any change. "See you tomorrow," she said, wrapping her scarf around the hair that had caught the men's attention. "Unless the snow's up to my armpits."

He got up fast. He didn't want Chandler coming into full view—there were several windows and he wasn't taking any chances that somebody else was still watching the restaurant. He met her halfway up the stairs.

"I told you I'd bring you your coat," she said.

"Two men just came in. Caucasian. Dark hair. Mid-forties. One was five-three, with an ugly scar on his chin. The other, five-ten. Recognize that description?"

"Not particularly, but why? Did they ask about me?" Her face had lost all its natural color.

"Not that I heard. But they focused on Jaylene at the counter. On her long brown hair."

Her hand went up to touch her own hair. "Yikes," she said weakly. "Doesn't fit the description of Marcus White. He's Asian."

"They were driving a black Suburban. I couldn't catch the license plate."

As soon as the words were out of his mouth, Chandler's head jerked up. He knew that somebody was behind him. He whirled, ready to fight.

It was Roxy.

"Those men asked if I'd seen a pretty young woman with long brown hair and emerald-green eyes like a cat."

Ethan felt his chest tighten. "What did you tell them?"

"I told them it didn't ring a bell."

"Thank you," Chandler whispered.

"I don't think you two are husband and wife and I don't think you're on your way to pick up your children. Neither one of you so much as gave that baby the time of day. And if you had your own kids, especially kids that you were missing, you'd have been all over that baby, wanting to know how old he was, talking about your own kids, things like that."

Ethan looked at Chandler. Busted.

Roxy would make one hell of a detective.

"We're not any danger to you," he said. "We believe those men have already tried to kill her twice."

Roxy stared at them. "Well, they don't know she's with you. Seemed to think she might be traveling alone."

That was good. Even if they saw his truck in the parking lot and had access to running the plate numbers, they wouldn't connect him to Chandler.

"Can we still stay here tonight?" he asked.

"I don't see why not," Roxy said. She turned. "This is kind of fun. Sort of like a Lifetime movie. Just make sure you don't bring trouble to my diner."

WHEN THEY GOT inside the room, Chandler sank down on the bed. Ethan remained standing. Molly jumped from the chair onto the bed and crowded up next to Chandler. She reached out a hand and rubbed it across the dog's shiny fur.

She felt sick. If she hadn't returned to the room, she would have been a sitting duck. She'd had her back to the door. An easy target for the goons that somebody had hired.

Ethan would have tried to protect her but it would have been two against one. He would have been hurt. Maybe killed.

She'd dragged him into something very dangerous and it was so unfair to him. He'd survived years of war only to come home to her problems, her danger.

"I'm sorry," she said.

"What?"

"I'm sorry that you're stuck in this stupid snowstorm, in this stupid little town, hiding away in this stupid little room with me." She waved a hand. "You should just go. Get out while you can. Maybe you can still make it back to the Donovan cabin. Maybe the road is open that direction."

He shook his head. "I doubt it. And even if it was, I'm not going anywhere."

"This isn't your fight. Nobody is out in the middle of the storm of the century looking for you."

"Just call the police. Blow the lid off this thing."

She considered it. "I just can't. It's my stepmother's

company. If I'm wrong and I've implicated either her or her company in a national scandal, she'll be furious. My dad may never forgive me." She paused. "I can't risk that."

"You could call the police and report the fact that two men are following you."

"True. But they haven't threatened me or harmed me. They didn't even ask for me by name, just a description that could fit a thousand other women."

"Emerald-green eyes like a cat," Ethan repeated. "That's not a thousand other women."

It was silly to feel warm and slightly off center because Ethan thought her eyes were special.

"What now?" she asked.

"I think I'm going to go shopping."

She frowned at him.

"You heard Roxy. They don't know anything about me. So I'm going to walk down to the drugstore and buy you some ibuprofen. I know you need it. And I'll get you your own toothbrush, too. I suspect you'd like that."

He was partially right. The pain reliever would be much appreciated. But she'd liked using his toothbrush. No way was she copping to that. She had planned to buy underwear, but asking him to do that for her would probably embarrass the heck out of him. She'd just keep sponging out what she had on.

"Ibuprofen and a toothbrush would be great," she said.

He studied her. "You won't leave the room while I'm gone?"

She shook her head.

"I'm leaving you in charge of Molly."

He said it as if he needed to give her a reason to stay

and be responsible. What was she going to do? Take off on foot in waist-high snow?

"While you're gone, I'm going to lie down and mentally rearrange my closet," she said. To prove her point, she lowered her back onto the bed and used one hand to fluff up the pillow under her head.

He smiled. "Rearrange your closet? That's the best you can do?"

"It always relaxes me. In my mind, I have everything color-coordinated, with like materials together. You knows, cottons, then knits, then everything denim. Of course, spring and summer on one side, fall and winter on the other. Shoes nicely stacked. Purses in a clear-sided tote."

He zipped up his coat. "I'm never going to understand women," he muttered, and rubbed Molly's head. "Take care of Chandler," he instructed.

He stepped away from the bed. Then, almost as if an afterthought, he stepped back and ran the pad of his thumb across the air bag burns on her cheeks and nose. "These look better," he said softly.

Her heart was racing in her chest. With one finger, she traced the scratch on his face that he'd gotten when they fell through the tree. His skin was so warm. "This, too," she whispered.

He didn't say anything for a long moment. Finally, he stepped away. "I'll be back."

HE SHOULD NOT have touched her. But he'd had this overwhelming need and he'd given in to it.

The skin on her face was soft. Sensual.

He suspected the rest of her would be the same.

When she'd reached up to touch the scratch on his face, he'd frozen.

And all he could think about was her touching him. Everywhere. It had taken about everything he had to walk out of the room.

Idiot. He strode faster, as fast as he could, in the middle of the road, hoping the cold air would clear his head. He watched for traffic but there was none. It was still tough going, but certainly easier than it would have been on the sidewalks. It was hard to tell how much snow had fallen since it was blowing around so much. He suspected a foot, maybe more.

When he got to Fantail Drugs, Jaylene was behind the counter. There was one other woman in the store, standing in front of a few shelves that had been dedicated to food. He saw cans of soup, boxes of cereal, sacks of potato chips, milk, beer and wine.

Appeared that Jaylene had all the basic food groups covered.

He found the short aisle that held the pain relievers and grabbed a big bottle. Then he went looking for the toothbrushes. Wanted a pink one but had to settle for white. He picked up some extra toothpaste while he was there.

On his way to the counter, he again got close to the food aisle. The chips were calling his name so he grabbed a big bag. And then he felt bad because he didn't know Chandler's snack of choice. His options were limited but he added a candy bar, red licorice and salted cashews to his stash.

He cradled his loot in one arm and snagged a bottle of wine with his free hand. When he got to the front counter, Jaylene smiled at him. "Is the ibuprofen just in case you drink too much wine?" she teased.

"Something like that," he said. "Some snow, huh?"

"Ridiculous. But that's how these storms work in the mountains. Fine one day and the next, snow everywhere. I saw you at Dot's. You're from out of town, aren't you?"

"Yeah. My wife and I got caught up in this mess and came here when the interstate got closed."

"You got a place to stay?"

"We do," he said, choosing not to elaborate.

The other customer came up and stood behind him. "Well, you're smart," the stranger said, jumping into the conversation.

"Hey, Marla," Jaylene said. "How's it going?"

"Oh, fine. I told Winston I needed a change of scenery for a few minutes." She looked at Ethan. "My husband and I own the gas station at the other end of Main Street. As usual, when it gets bad, it's just usually us, Fantail's and Dot's that manage to stay open."

"I suppose your being open is pretty helpful for the people who need gas," Ethan said.

"Yeah. But it seems as if a storm like this blows some strange folk in. I had two odd ducks stop by just before I came here. They asked whether I'd seen some woman. I hadn't, of course. Nobody is out today. Anyway, they filled up their tank, bought four packs of cigarettes and a couple cans of oil. Last I saw, they were headed out of town although I don't know where the heck they think they're going to get to. They had a big four-wheel-drive vehicle but even those things get stuck in this kind of snow. Someone will probably find them next spring upside down in one of the gullies."

One could only hope. Ethan took his change from

Jaylene and grabbed the white plastic sack. "Thanks very much."

He walked back to Dot's. The diner was empty and Roxy was sitting at the counter, reading a magazine.

"Get what you needed?" she asked.

"Yes." He glanced at the television, which Roxy had turned up loud since there were no customers. The newscaster was droning on about the first blizzard of the season. The interstate was still closed and they were asking everyone to stay off all other roads, that emergency crews were not able to respond.

"It's bad," she said. "Snow like this always makes it seem as if time has stopped because the world sort of just shuts down."

Time hadn't stopped, but there was something odd about it. It had only been about eighteen hours since he'd followed Molly into the woods and stumbled upon Chandler hanging in the trees.

Not such a long time.

But yet he felt a familiarity with Chandler that he hadn't felt with people that he'd served with for ten years.

Maybe it was because he'd known her as a child. Maybe it was because she had the same spirit and spunk that Mack always demonstrated, and that Ethan had always admired.

Maybe it was because she wore pretty underwear, her skin was soft and her hair smelled delicious?

"Are you going to close earlier than eight?" Ethan asked.

"I might close a little earlier if nobody else comes in. You want me to make you up some sandwiches for dinner, just in case?"

"That might be good." He set his plastic sack down

on the counter. He still had the bread and peanut butter from his own supplies but there was no need to resort to that if they could get something better.

"How about some chicken salad on wheat, fruit and maybe a couple pieces of chocolate cake?" Roxy asked.

Ethan remembered the look on Chandler's face when she'd dug into her pie. "Sure. Sounds perfect," he said.

It took Roxy less than five minutes to assemble the to-go order. She put it all in a small insulated bag that she pulled from underneath the counter. "Here. This will keep it cold until you are ready to eat it. Just leave the bag in the room when you leave."

Ethan pulled out forty bucks and threw it on the counter.

"That's way too much," she said.

He waved his hand. "It's not really enough."

She stared at him. "I hope everything works out for you and your woman. I'm a pretty good judge of character and you two look like good people."

Your woman.

Chandler was willing to be.

No strings attached.

And he could feel his moral high ground crumbling every time he glanced in her direction.

WHEN HE GOT to the room, she was sleeping. He stood and watched her for several minutes, marveling at how beautiful she was. How many men had been infatuated with her? How many had tried in vain to earn her interest?

But somehow she'd remained unattached.

As if she was waiting for him.

Dream on.

He lay down on the floor and closed his own eyes, waking sometime later when he heard her groan.

He sprang up.

There was no danger. She was still asleep. Or mostly so. Her eyes were still closed and her breathing deep, but she was rubbing her sore shoulder.

"Chandler, wake up. You need to take some pain relievers. Chandler," he said again, a little louder.

One pretty eye opened. "What?"

He opened the sack, pulled out the medication, opened the bottle and shook two pills into his palm. He handed them to her along with a bottle of water. "Here."

She took a small sip of water and then swallowed the pills. Then another big drink. "Thanks."

"How bad is the pain?" he asked.

"It's okay. I think I might have rolled over onto it. Now that I'm awake, it's going to be hard to go back to sleep."

It drove him crazy that she was hurting. "Want to play cards?" he asked.

She tilted her head. "Poker?"

"Sure."

"What else is in the sack?"

He pulled out the chips, the candy, the cashews. "I wasn't sure what you liked."

"All of it. First hand is for the licorice."

"So that's how it is. This is serious." He opened his duffel and pulled out the deck of cards.

She sat up in the bed and scooted back so that her spine rested against the headboard. She motioned for him to hand her the cards. When he did, she shuffled the deck, fanning the cards out on the bed like some Vegas dealer.

"Who taught you how to play cards?"

"You, Mack and Brody. Then my dad. And then finally, my college roommate. I think she majored in poker and minored in shopping. Fun girl."

She put the cards down and motioned for him to cut. He did. "Deuces wild," she said, right before she starting dealing.

She won the licorice with a queen-high straight.

He held on to the potato chips with a full house, tens and threes.

She snatched up the salted cashews after winning the next hand with a pair of aces.

He got the candy bar with four sevens.

She won the wine with two pairs, kings and fives. There was a brief moment of panic before she realized it had a screw top, not a cork. She got plastic cups out of the bathroom and poured a glass for each of them.

He opened the chips and offered her some.

"Delicious," she said.

Gorgeous, he thought.

She ripped open the seal of the salted cashews. "I love these."

He felt good that he'd guessed right. "As much as a bacon, egg and cheese sandwich?"

She chewed and considered. "You know why I love that sandwich so much?" she asked, her voice suddenly serious.

He shook his head.

"A week after my mom died, I had to go back to school. I was in second grade. I got up and got dressed and when I went downstairs, my dad was standing at the stove. And I could tell that he'd been crying. But he turned to me and he made himself smile. He said,

'Chandler, I may not make it exactly like your mom did but I'll do my best. Don't you worry, honey, I'm going to take care of you. We're going to take care of each other.'"

Ethan could feel his throat tighten. "You and your dad will find your way back to each other."

Chandler didn't answer. She simply took a big drink of her wine. Finally, she put her empty glass down.

"We're out of items to win," she said brightly.

He could tell that she was making the effort to get past the past few minutes. "Not true." He opened the insulated bag that Roxy had packed and showed it to her. "Chicken salad sandwiches. Fruit salad. Chocolate cake."

She looked closer at the cake. "Chocolate is sort of sacred. I'd feel bad if I won your piece. We can't bet on that."

"We played over a candy bar. That had chocolate in it."

She shook her head. "But this is homemade chocolate *cake*. With chocolate icing and what looks to be a layer of chocolate mousse in the middle. Comparing this to the candy bar is like comparing ice cream to frozen yogurt. Similar but definitely not the same." She poured herself another glass of wine.

Ethan looked around the room, searching for something of value. "Peanut butter and bread?" he asked. "I can get them out of the truck."

She shook her head, then lifted her chin. "How about strip poker?"

Chapter Nine

"No." The word hadn't exploded out of his mouth but pretty darn close. What was she thinking?

"Come on," she said. "We're pretty evenly matched. If we lose, we take off something. But if we win, we get to put it back on. In fact, we can bank points to offset future losses. For example, if you win three in a row and you don't have anything to put back on, you can bank those points to cover your next three losses."

It was the craziest game of poker he'd ever played. But her eyes were shining again and she seemed to have moved past her momentary unhappiness.

He couldn't believe he was about to agree to this insanity.

He handed her the cards. "Your deal."

She got off the bed, slipped on her shoes, and put on her jacket. Then she got back on the bed and picked up the cards.

"Hedging your bets," he said.

"Oh, no. I was just chilly." She laughed.

"Right." He picked up his cards and had nothing. He threw down three and she dealt replacement cards. He ended up with a pair of jacks.

It wasn't enough to beat her three fours. He took off a shoe.

The game went back and forth for forty minutes, with both of them taking off and putting back on shoes and socks and belts. They drank their wine, emptying the bottle. Chandler ate half her piece of cake; Ethan focused on the potato chips.

It was fun.

Up until the point that Chandler lost four hands in a row. She took off both shoes and both socks.

"Your feet are going to get cold," he teased, dealing the cards.

Then his full house, sixes and twos, beat her two pairs. She took off her jacket.

On the next hand, he was dealt a flush. A hand of hearts. And he considered throwing several in, to make sure that he lost the hand. He had the tips of his fingers on the cards but he couldn't make himself do it.

"I'll hold with what I've got," he said.

She took three cards.

"Flush," he said, laying down his hand on the bed-spread.

She chewed her bottom lip. "Pair of fives," she said.

Their eyes met. And she slowly started to unbutton her blouse.

"Look," he said. "You don't have to—"

"Play by the rules? I do," she added softly.

She got to the last button and he realized that he was holding his breath. And it came out in a rush when she took off the cotton shirt in one smooth movement.

He'd seen her bra before. But still, he wasn't prepared for the sight of her perfectly round breasts covered by the little bit of lace and silk.

Her skin was pale, with just a slight rosy hue.

"Deal," she said.

No, his mind silently screamed. He was playing with fire. He shuffled the cards and realized that his hands were shaking.

He dealt himself a pair of threes. When it came time to discard, he threw them in. She was going to get to put her shirt back on.

She threw in three cards and he dealt her the replacements.

"I've got nothing," he said, laying down his hand.

"Me either."

He looked to see who had the high card. He had an ace. She had a king.

She started to unzip her jeans. He reached out a hand to stop her. "Look, Chandler, we have to stop."

She shook her head and within seconds, she was sitting before him in her dark blue underwear. And he could not keep his eyes off her.

She picked up the cards to deal. He grabbed her wrist. Her skin was warm and soft. "No," he said.

She dealt the hand.

He looked at his cards and shook his head when she asked if he wanted any cards. "I'll hold on this," he said, his voice cracking.

"Me, too."

The room felt hot and small and when he looked out the window, all he saw was white everywhere. It felt as if he and Chandler McCann were the only people in the world. It felt right.

He turned his cards over. Full house, kings and fours. She flipped her cards over, one at a time. Two pairs, tens and threes.

"Full house beats two pairs most days," he said softly.

"Most days," she repeated as she unsnapped her bra.

And her beautiful breasts were there for the taking, with nipples the loveliest shade of rose.

And he desperately wanted her.

He moved fast, sending the cards flying off the bed.

"Game over," he said, right before he started taking off his own shirt.

HE UNDRESSED WITH frightening efficiency, as if to say that once he'd made up his mind, nothing was stopping him.

It was an exhilarating feeling.

And when he stood before her in all his splendid glory, she felt a surge of lust run through her body. She'd known she wanted this, but now that it was truly happening, she wanted it with an intensity that was all-consuming.

She started to take off her panties.

He held up a finger. "Let me."

And he did. With his teeth.

Skimming and nipping and dragging his hot tongue against her needy, quivering body.

And she'd thought that he might take her quickly. But once she was naked and up tight against him, he seemed to settle down, settle in.

With both of them on their sides, he took his hands and framed her face. And then he kissed her. Gently. Languidly. As if she were the precious dessert that he had coveted for a very long time.

His tongue was in her mouth and she was arching against his body. It was perfect.

And the kisses went on for a very long time until finally, he rolled her on her back, bent his head and took her nipple in his mouth.

She lifted her hips.

"Not yet," he murmured.

She was going to implode.

He kissed and licked his way down her body until finally his mouth settled on her. And in minutes, she was shaking with need.

Finally, he lifted his head. His eyes were dark, his face serious. "I've got condoms in my bag."

She shook her head. "I'm on the pill to regulate my periods. I'm healthy," she added.

"Me, too," he said, his tone guttural. He used his hands to spread her legs wide. And then he was inside, gently pushing, letting her adjust, making sure it was just right.

And then he started to move.

And it was really just seconds before she came with a rush so intense that she was surprised she didn't pass out. She arched her back, taking him deeper.

"Watch your shoulder," he warned.

There was no pain anywhere. Only pleasure.

When her climax was over, he held her, letting her rest. "Okay?" he asked after a moment.

"That was better than cake," she whispered, her lips close to his shoulder.

He chuckled. "Then, hang on, honey," he said, his voice suddenly hoarse. He started to move. Long strokes in and out. He cupped his hands under her thighs, opening her, and she felt him even deeper.

It was erotic and wonderful and while it didn't seem possible, she felt her need build again. And when he pressed his hand between them, touching her most sensitive parts, she exploded one more time.

Then, with a growl close to her ear, he pounded into

her, skin slapping against skin, until he threw his head back and emptied himself inside her.

ETHAN WOKE UP when it was dark outside. The blinds were still open and he could see that it had finally stopped snowing. He thought they'd probably been sleeping for a couple hours.

Making love to Chandler McCann had been the most intense experience of his life. More intense than flying night missions over enemy territory. More intense than righting his helicopter after wind caught the blades wrong.

She was beautiful. After he'd come inside of her, he'd caught his breath, then managed to pull out and get cleaned up. Then he'd crawled back into bed, tucked her against his body, her back to his front, and they'd slept.

She was still sleeping. He wrapped his hand around her long hair and moved it to the side. Then he brushed his lips across her shoulder.

She moaned.

He nibbled on her ear.

She stretched, her pretty body arching slightly.

He licked her neck.

Her eyes were open now. She pressed her sexy bottom up against him.

He pushed her gently to her stomach and spread her legs. And then he took her from behind.

She was hot and wet and when she pressed back against him and came in jerky spasms, he couldn't control his reaction. He pounded into her and when he came, he collapsed on her, rolling them just enough to the side to keep his weight off her.

"Good evening to you, too," she said several minutes later.

He only had the energy to smile.

"What time is it?" she asked.

He lifted his wrist. "Just after seven. Are you hungry?"

She scooted up in bed and he saw her wince slightly. "Are you okay?"

"I'm fabulous," she said. "I just put a little too much weight on my shoulder."

"You could probably take some more ibuprofen."

"I will. In a minute." She settled back into his arms.

It was dark outside but there was so much snow everywhere that there was a soft grayness to the evening. The trees, some with leaves that had not yet fallen, were heavy with snow.

What was it Roxy had said? *Snow like this always makes it seem as if time has stopped.* To him, it made it seem as if life were really a Larry Donovan novel. That somehow, some way, the rest of the world had ended and the only survivors were Chandler and him.

And it was okay.

"Whatcha thinking about?" Chandler asked.

"The quiet," he replied, willing to only tell a half-truth.

"The cabin was quiet, too."

"Yeah, but I'd only been there a few weeks. I was still getting used to it."

"War isn't quiet?"

War was sometimes tedious and even boring because there was always a good amount of waiting. War was also interesting and complicated and actions begot spontaneous reactions.

"War can be quiet. Or noisy as hell."

It had been everything that was important to him.

But then came Operation Wind Jammer.

Had the mission gone off without a hitch, lots of important people, people at the very top, would have been drowning in accolades. The press would have been *impressed* and a few stars might have been added to the jackets of his superior officers.

It might even have been spectacular. The capture of enemies that had eluded U.S. forces for nearly a decade.

A final stake in the ground, if you will.

But it had gone badly. And the enemy had been ready for them. And even though he and the others had regrouped quickly, they'd lost eight. Embedded reporters had been critical and the twenty-four-hour news stations had reported at great length about a twenty-first-century army that had been bested by a bunch of ragtag insurgent rebels.

He'd mourned the loss of his fellow soldiers and had been ill-prepared when suddenly there was a JAG officer at his door informing him he was under investigation. Ugly, ugly words. And after months of scrutiny and months of answering the same damn questions over and over again, he'd been cleared. They'd pulled him off the desk duty that they'd assigned him to and let him back in the helicopter.

But he'd decided it was time to leave for good.

"My dad thought it was cool that you were flying helicopters," Chandler said.

He'd enlisted right out of high school, hadn't really known what he wanted to do but had been certain that he wasn't going to stay in some small town in Oregon and work at the local factory where his stepfather worked.

Then he'd heard about flight school and had worked his butt off, making sure that he was on the short list of candidates. He wouldn't have denied that it mattered a great deal because Baker McCann had always loved helicopters. That, combined with the fact that he really believed it was a way that he could help his country win a crazy war in a faraway place, was enough to have him scramble for a spot on the exclusive list of flight school participants.

He'd done well. Had a natural affinity for flying and had quickly risen through the ranks, earning promotion after promotion, and finally, fourteen years in, had achieved his goal of becoming a standardization pilot. In that role he was responsible for working with hundreds of other pilots, assessing their competencies, ensuring that skills remained sharp, that the pilots in his brigade were simply the best. With his last promotion to a CW5, he'd been at the top of his game.

And then one night, in a dusty little town in a country where the war was supposed to be over, it had gone south. Helicopters had taken fire. More hits than could have reasonably been assembled unless the enemy had been waiting for them. Special Forces troops had been left unprotected. Casualties had mounted.

The rumbling started soon after. Information had to have been leaked. It was a relatively short list of people who had been in the know.

Unfortunately, his name had been on that list.

And for some reason, at the top of that list.

He pulled away from Chandler and sat up in bed, his back to her. "We should probably get dressed."

He could feel her stretch. "You're right. I'm going to

use the bathroom first." She scooted off the bed, stopped long enough to grab her clothes and left the room.

He continued to sit on the bed for several minutes. He was grateful that she hadn't probed about his military service, hadn't wanted to know more about what had prompted his decision to leave.

After a minute, he got up and quickly dressed. Then he opened the bag that Roxy had packed. Everything was still nice and cold. On the bed, he made a quick picnic. A sandwich and a dish of fruit for each of them. Then he split his piece of cake in half since Chandler had already eaten most of her piece. He handed out the plastic silverware and napkins that Roxy had thrown in.

He looked up when she opened the bathroom door fully dressed. She smiled when she saw the cake. She walked over to the window and lifted the edge of the blind. "It stopped snowing," she said, turning to look at him. Her eyes were serious.

He wished he could make this whole damn mess go away for her. He couldn't do that, but he could get her to Denver, help her get the proof she needed and then take her away for about two weeks to a tropical island where they could drink rum and make love all day. "It doesn't mean the road is open," he said. "But I suspect it will be shortly."

"If you don't mind, can we eat and then take off? I'd like to get ahead of those men who were looking for me."

He intended to keep his gun handy. If those men so much as looked in Chandler's direction, he would be prepared.

They ate in silence, each lost in their own thoughts. Was it possible that Chandler was regretting what had happened between them earlier? Had the wine gotten to her head? Had she gotten carried away with the moment and now, faced with the reality of what was ahead of her, was she regretting the impulse to make love? What was it she'd said? *I can be a little impulsive at times.*

"Penny for your thoughts."

She chewed and swallowed. "I'm sorry, I'm poor company."

"You're fine," he assured her. "Was...was this fine?" He waved his hand toward the tangled bed linens.

"I have a confession," she said.

He didn't want to hear it. Not if it was going to change anything about what had just happened. "What's that?" he asked, his throat tight.

"I threw away three nines."

"Huh?"

"On the hand after the one where I lost my shirt. No pun intended," she added. "I purposely threw away three nines so that I'd lose the hand. I figured getting undressed was the best chance I'd have of convincing you to take me to bed. I tricked you."

He assessed her. She didn't look upset or even apologetic. She looked relaxed. Content. And he felt his heart start to beat normally again.

He reached over and stabbed a bite of her cake. "You owe me this," he said.

"I suppose I do," she agreed. "I'm happy to pay up in other ways, too." She licked her lips and stared at his zipper.

And he could feel his body respond. "If I take you up on that, we might not get out of here until morning."

She sighed. "We have to go."

As much as he hated it, she was right. "The way I

see it, you still owe me a cherry pie with vanilla ice cream. I guess I could add this most recent offer to the list."

There was a smile in her pretty eyes. "You do that."

Chapter Ten

It didn't take them long to pack up. When they walked out of the small bedroom, Chandler took a moment to study the space. So much had happened since they'd entered it early this morning. Would Dot's still be here the next time she came through? It could be years. Maybe Dot's would be but Roxy might have moved on. Would she be able to sit at the counter, next to different men in the same brown coveralls, and eat a piece of pie?

Would she be alone?

"Ready?" Ethan asked.

She nodded, closed the door behind her and followed him down the stairs. After Ethan opened the door that led to the parking lot, he paused and Chandler saw him look from side to side. Assessing. Judging.

He evidently thought it looked safe enough because he motioned for her to follow him. With his broad shoulders out of her way, she could see that his truck was the only vehicle in the lot. It was a big lump of white with little patches of black peeking through.

The lot hadn't been plowed. However, the street had. The streetlights made it easy enough to see that the snowplow had made at least one pass through. She hoped that meant that they would be able to get back to the interstate and ultimately get to Denver.

Ethan started the truck and Chandler and Molly got inside while he cleaned off the windows. It took several minutes because the snow was many inches deep. By the time Ethan opened the door again, the interior was starting to get warm.

"Getting out of this lot may be the toughest part," Ethan said. He put the truck in Drive and they started moving.

Chandler let out the breath she'd been holding. "I wish we could buy gas before we get back on the road."

"I do, too," Ethan said. "I think I'll drive that direction just to see if the gas station is still open."

It wasn't.

"How much gas do we have?"

"A little less than half a tank. We'll just have to watch it closely."

It was one more thing in a list of things to worry about. But for right now, they were back on the road. She needed to focus on the positive. And maybe reflect on the amazing. *Dear Diary, this afternoon I had sex with Ethan Moore.*

The small book with its feeble little lock would have spontaneously combusted!

Sort of like she'd done. Multiple times.

And still it wasn't enough. Maybe when she and Ethan got back to Denver and this mess was resolved, they—

"Just one lane open," Ethan said, interrupting her thoughts.

Just as well, she rationalized. She had no business thinking about that right now. She needed to stay focused. "I hope we don't meet anyone," she said.

Fortunately, they didn't. And when they got to the interstate, a single lane on each side of the yellow line was open, with snow piled high on the side. It was as if they were driving through a tunnel.

Five miles into their trip, they saw a car in the opposing lane. Chandler took it as a good sign. Surely traffic wouldn't be coming from the other direction if the road was blocked.

"What happens when we get to Denver?" Ethan asked.

"I appreciate your positive attitude. Not *if* we get to Denver but rather, *when.*"

"We'll get there," he said, his tone certain. "If it keeps going like this, maybe by midnight."

"I need to get inside the building."

"Tell me about Linder Automation."

"We're located in a huge industrial park. We occupy the third and fourth floors of a six-story building. There's a twenty-four-hour guard at the front desk and employees access their own work area with card swipes."

"What area of the building do you need to get into?"

She thought about that. "Any area that has a computer. I just need to be able to sign on to our network so that I can look at some data that would be on one of our backup servers."

"What kind of data?"

"I told you that I was confident that both Marcus White and my stepmother had viewed the twelve screens that contained the product specifications. There is an immense amount of data in these twelve different files. We've always felt pretty good about the security of the information because the files can't be downloaded— there's a code in the background that prevents that. But

I remembered," she said, shrugging a little, "too late, of course, that somebody could do an electronic screen print of the data."

"So let's assume one of them did a screen print. How does that help you?"

"It wouldn't be just one screen print or even twelve screen prints. This is complex data, with formulas behind formulas. I don't know for sure but I'll bet they would have needed to do over a hundred screen prints to get all the data. And if they're selling this data, I don't think they're selling it to someone who only wants part of the equation."

"I'm sure," he said drily. "So you think they printed over a hundred screenshots and handed those over to the enemy?"

"Yes. And I think those pieces of paper are long gone. But every time they pushed the button to do a screenshot, a temporary electronic file would have been generated. Now, both Marcus and my stepmother would know how to delete those temporary files. That's pretty simple. But what I'm counting on is that neither one of them knows that we have a server that captures and indexes all temporary print files. I built it about two months ago."

"Why?"

"One of my good friends at Linder is getting married. It's been a whirlwind relationship but I'm not worried because her fiancé is a great guy. However, less than nine months ago, she was dating someone else who happens to also work at Linder. They broke up after she realized that he was sleeping with someone else while he was dating her."

"Given what you told me about Christivo, I imagine you're sensitive to those kinds of situations."

"You think?" She smiled. "Anyway, about three months ago, he became her boss. She's a wonderful employee but she thinks that he's going to try to make it difficult for her to be successful. Not in any overt way, of course, just subtle stuff."

"Could happen. But still not getting how this goes with temporary print files being captured on a server."

"She works two jobs. So she needs to use her lunch hours to plan her wedding. She scours online bridal magazines, food magazines, et cetera. Whenever she sees something that she likes, she uses the print screen function, which creates the temporary electronic file, but she doesn't actually print the page. She's afraid to. They work in the same area and he might pick it up off the printer before she could get to it. If he saw something like that, he'd have a reason to have somebody from the IT staff look at her computer activity. If there was lots of wedding stuff, he could probably make the case that she's using work time."

"Jerk," Ethan said.

"Exactly. Even though he was going out on her, he's pretty jealous that she found someone and that they're getting married so quickly. I told her not to worry about saving the pictures or emailing them to her personal email account, that I would set up a program where I captured all her print screen activity. Then when she's ready, it would be a simple download."

"But you're capturing everyone's?"

"Yes. I realized that when I saw how big the file was getting. It was on my list to fix but I had more important projects at work and just hadn't gotten to it. The only harm was that it was using server space but we have plenty of that so I wasn't too concerned."

"So you need to access this server and download whatever is on it. How long will that take?"

"Not long once I'm in the building. Five to ten minutes, maybe."

"You said there was a guard 24/7 at the front door. Any other entrances?"

"There are some side doors and a back door to the building, but none of them have card swipes. They're mostly used as emergency exits. Everybody who works in that building has to come past the guard. We're not the only government contractor there. Security is pretty tight. There's a gate that everybody has to pass through. The security guard hits a button to raise a red entrance bar once he's seen your badge."

"Then how do you propose to get in?"

"I've been thinking about that. All the tenants in the building use the same cleaning company. I guess it's part of the lease agreement. People come in at night and clean. They all have to have rigid background checks to be in the building, and the cleaning company guarantees that they are never there unsupervised."

"Still not getting it."

"They don't exactly live up to their guarantee. The supervisors are there. But mostly hanging out in the office and hanging all over each other. There are two night supervisors, and they are both married to other people who probably have no idea that the missus and the mister are getting more than a paycheck at work. They sometimes don't come out of the office for hours. I work at night a couple times a month because it's the best time to do system maintenance. I know the routine. They stand in the hall when the workers arrive, hand out assignments and then disappear."

"So you intend to be part of the cleaning crew? Aren't they going to be suspicious when you show up for work and they didn't hire you?"

"I don't think they do the hiring. That all gets done out of some corporate office. I was there one night when a new person started. It was pretty clear they'd never met her before."

"It sounds as if it could work. But you said earlier that everybody needs a badge to get past the security guard."

"That's the part I haven't quite figured out."

He was quiet for a minute and she waited for him to drill holes in her plan.

"You'll think of something," he said finally, his voice soft, yet confident.

And she fell a little bit more in love with Ethan Moore.

THEY HIT DENVER a little after midnight. The streets had been plowed and while it was piled high on the edges of the road, it was apparent that the city had not gotten as much snowfall as the mountains. The few cars that were out were moving around easily.

"I guess going to my house is out of the question," Chandler said, her voice heavy with regret.

That wouldn't be smart. It was anyone's guess who might be watching the house. "Do you need something?"

"Clean clothes."

"You still look good in those," he said, smiling at her.

She shook her head. "Turn at that next light. There's a wannabe-Walmart drugstore about a mile up. They have a bunch of different things. I can get something there."

He found the store without any trouble. There were at least fifteen cars in the parking lot, proving that people really did shop at any time of the day or night. He pulled into a space, threw the truck into Park and pulled the keys. "What do you want me to get you?" he asked.

She frowned at him. "I want to go in."

It could be dangerous. They were back in her hometown. "Where do you live from here?"

"About twenty-five minutes east."

"Where is Linder Automation from here?"

"Twenty minutes north."

"You don't normally shop here?" he asked.

"No. I've never been inside. There are stores much closer to my house. The guy who does my taxes lives about three blocks from here. That's how I knew the store was here."

It wasn't her neighborhood and it wasn't near her work. Plus it was after midnight. The likelihood that she would see anyone she knew was very small.

"Okay. But we make it fast."

"No problem. I just want to grab some yoga pants and a T-shirt. Something comfortable. And maybe an inexpensive pair of shoes. The ones I have on have had it."

He pulled out his wallet and handed her two one-hundred-dollar bills. "Will this cover it?"

She held the bills between her index finger and her thumb, as if they were tainted. "I wish I didn't have to keep taking your money."

"I don't think you have a choice."

She shook her head. "I hate this."

"It will be over soon. Come on, let's go."

They walked into the store. It was warm and brightly lit. There were two female clerks, each at a cash register, neither with customers, keeping themselves occupied by chatting. There was a young man on a machine that was quietly cleaning the tile floor.

Chandler paused, read the suspended aisle signs and headed toward the rear of the store. He followed. It took her less than three minutes to select some black pants and two T-shirts, one black, one red. Then, with a quick look over her shoulder, she walked over to the lingerie aisles.

And damn, in the middle of some stupid store, he got all hot and bothered as she ran her hands across a rack full of bras.

He was toast.

Knew it.

And the back of his throat got tight when he found himself wondering what Mack and Baker McCann would have to say. Would they be happy? Would they think he was good enough for Chandler? Would they want to kick his ass for getting involved with her when he had his own problems to deal with?

Chandler grabbed a matching bra and panty set. Light yellow. He'd always loved yellow.

She led him over to the shoe department. He thought maybe she'd go for another pair of loafers, but she quickly settled on a pair of ankle boots with a solid half-inch heel. She sat down to try them on. They seemed to fit.

She took them off, put them back in the box and smiled up at him. "These will work. See? I'm really a very fast shopper."

"Got to love a woman who knows what she wants."

She jerked her head down, breaking eye contact, so quickly that he was surprised she didn't put her spine out of alignment. Then she got busy putting her loafers back on.

Love a woman. It had been an off-the-cuff remark.

Hadn't it? His brain might be temporarily scrambled but that didn't mean he was in love.

She picked up her armload of purchases and started walking.

She was going to let his comment go.

He wasn't sure if he was relieved or irritated that she didn't want to talk about it. Didn't women want to talk about everything? Analyze everything? Dissect? Pick?

Great. He had to find the *one* who was just going to *let it go,* like water running off her back.

On the way to the cash register, she made a detour into the electronics section. She picked up an eight-gigabyte flash drive. It was about the size of Ethan's thumbnail. Then, the next aisle over, she scooped up a cell phone with a prepaid calling card that would last six hours.

When they got to the cash register, both clerks had customers in line. Chandler stood behind a woman who appeared to be preparing for a paper shortage. She was buying multiples of paper towels, toilet paper, napkins and brown lunch bags.

It took a minute for the clerk to get it all bagged up. Then Chandler stepped forward. It took just a minute to complete the transaction. As they walked out of the store, Chandler handed him the change.

"Keep it," he said.

She didn't say anything. Just stuffed the bills into her jeans pocket.

Should he apologize for making her uncomfortable? Should he make a joke about it?

He didn't do either. Just got in his truck, petted Molly, who had been patiently waiting for them, and waited for Chandler to get her seat belt buckled.

She immediately got busy taking the phone out of its plastic case. "Do you want to carry the phone or do you want me to?" she asked.

"Keep it," he repeated. He wanted her to have all the protection she could get. "Are you going to call Mack?"

She shook her head. "Not yet. I hate that he'll be worried but we're so close now. When I have the proof, one way or the other, then I'll call him. In an hour or two, we should know. I'll have the evidence."

He pulled out of the lot and Chandler pointed toward the road that they'd come in on. "If you follow this road and turn left at the third light, we'll be headed toward Linder Automation."

He did as instructed. Traffic was still light although there was a set of lights behind him. They drove in silence. The first light was red and he stopped. The only sound in the truck was Molly's breathing.

The second light was green and he breezed through. At the third light, he prepared to turn left. And noted that the car behind him made the same turn.

"In about a mile, you'll have to make another left-hand turn. The street is Chillicothe."

The street would have been a bustling business area during the day, but at one o'clock in the morning, there was very little activity. So where the hell was the driver behind him headed?

It could have been a million places, but Ethan couldn't shake the feeling that something was wrong. And his gut had saved his life more than once in combat. He'd known just when to pull up or pull out of a flight pattern.

"Hang on," he said. He accelerated just slightly, putting some distance between his truck and the vehicle behind them. Then he made a quick right-hand turn onto a side street.

"What?" Chandler squealed.

The side street had been plowed but not as well as the main road. The pavement was still snow-covered. The back end of the truck slid and his tires grabbed.

He wasn't worried about that. He was watching the rearview mirror.

The car behind him made the same turn.

Out of a million possible places, what were the chances it was on this street?

Not many.

"I think we've got company." He continued to drive. "Do you know where this street leads to?"

"I'm not sure. Some of these side streets connect the two main roads that head north. I don't know if this is one of them or if it's a dead end somewhere up here."

He hoped not.

She turned in her seat to look at the vehicle behind them. "Who is that? Is it the men who came to Dot's?"

Not unless they'd changed vehicles. This was a light-colored midsize car. He could tell that from the position of its lights and the glimpse he'd caught in the mirror as it had rounded the corner. He hadn't been able to see who was driving or how many were in the car.

He remembered what the woman from the gas station had said about the men buying oil. Had they known that their vehicle was in bad shape? Had they somehow switched it? "I don't know," he said. "It's not an SUV." The car had dropped back just a little. "I think we picked them up when we were leaving the store. Did you see anybody in there that you recognized?"

"No. I would have said something."

Yeah, but they'd both been distracted because he'd decided to awkwardly profess his love in the shoe aisle. "I'm going to try to lose them," he said. "I'd rather do that than force a confrontation right now."

"Good plan," she said, her voice tight. She wrapped an arm around Molly, anchoring the dog next to her side.

He picked up his speed. It was a residential street and there were cars parked on one side and snow piled up on the other, making the path through a narrow one. Five blocks in, there was a stop sign. He approached, looked both directions to make sure that there was nobody coming and blew through the intersection without stopping. When the vehicle behind him did the same and started to edge closer, he pressed the accelerator.

They were traveling much too fast on the snow-covered street. Up ahead, he saw a traffic signal and assumed that was the main road. The light was green.

He intended to make that light. "Hang on."

He made the turn just as the light went from yellow to red.

And let out a breath when the car behind him got stopped by cross traffic. But since there were only a couple of cars, Ethan knew it was a brief reprieve.

He pressed down on the accelerator, wanting to put distance between the two vehicles.

Then he took a quick right, drove one block, turned left, left again, then right, doing a haphazard zigzag. He saw what he thought might work and turned into a parking lot. It was some type of industrial building and there were lots of fresh tracks in and out of the parking lot. There was a road that led behind the building. It was plowed. Ethan took it.

And suddenly they were behind the brick building, effectively hidden from any traffic that might wander by.

He turned off the engine. Once again, the only sound in the truck was Molly's breathing.

After a minute, Chandler turned to him. "Well, that was fun," she said, her voice cracking at the end.

More than ever, he appreciated her spirit.

"I'm sure I didn't recognize anybody in the store," she said. "And the only person in the store who seemed to pay any attention to us was looking at you, not at me."

Chapter Eleven

"What?"

Molly whined, not used to hearing that tone of voice. He made a deliberate effort to modify it. "What did you say?" he asked.

"When we were standing in line, waiting to pay, there was a man getting checked out in the other lane. For just a second, I thought he was looking at you oddly. As if he was very angry about something. Then I figured he was mad because the cashier at his register was making a big deal about folding the one customer's clothes just right before putting them in the bag."

Her words made him cold. Had it been someone he'd served with? Someone who thought the rumors about him were true? Someone who really thought that he'd have sold out his fellow soldiers?

Impossible. He'd have recognized the person.

But people changed. Grew their hair out. Got contacts. Gained or lost weight.

Had Chandler been in danger because of him? Had she been in danger since the beginning because of him? Had the incident at the cabin been a violent attack against him?

Had she almost died because of him?

He'd considered the possibility, but she'd been so confident that it was because of her, he'd willingly gone down that path and kept his own demons hidden.

He should tell her the truth. Now. Tell her all the reasons why it was a mistake to get involved with him.

But he kept his mouth shut.

How could he risk losing her when he'd just found her? And he surely wouldn't risk her executing her plan to break into Linder Automation on her own, which she'd certainly do after she sent him away. She needed backup. Someone to protect her.

He couldn't bear it if she thought the ugly rumors were true. Ethan Moore, a traitor.

There was adrenaline pumping through his veins— maybe it was the car chase, maybe it was the suspense of not knowing who it might have been, maybe it was the look in her striking green eyes. Whatever, he felt on fire. A little reckless.

And he had a blinding need to hold Chandler tight, to claim her as his. To cement the relationship so that it couldn't be undone by ugly accusations and vicious lies.

But he held himself in check. He thought they were safe but he wasn't going to take a chance on the car doubling back and somehow finding them behind the building.

"Chandler?"

"Yes?"

He could hear the question in her response. The tension in the truck was palpable.

"You should probably change into your new clothes here," he said.

CHANDLER REACHED FOR the bag that had her new clothes and her boots. She put on the new underwear, the black yoga pants and the black T-shirt. When she finished putting on her new black boots, she realized that Ethan was watching her.

"What?" she asked.

He shook his head. "Nothing."

She could see the want in his eyes. It made her feel good. She wished she didn't have this ugliness to deal with. Wished she and Ethan could find a nice hotel room and spend about a week there, getting to know one another. She wanted to make love to him, again and again.

But she could not turn back now. She had to finish what she'd started, what someone else had really started.

"We should go," she said. "At Linder Automation, we work forty-five hours a week. That's five nine-hour days with a half-hour lunch. And there are two shifts. The first shift works from eight in the morning until five-thirty at night. To allow for some crossover between shifts, the second shift starts at five in the afternoon and goes until two-thirty. Everybody has to be out of the building by three at the latest. The night cleaning crew begins work at three-thirty in the morning and is out of the building by six-thirty."

She looked at her watch. "I thought of a way to get in. Don't know if it will work but it's the best I can come up with."

"Let's hear it."

"From what I recall, there are usually six to eight people on the cleaning crew. More women than men. A van brings a group of them to work. A few others drive their own cars and park in a lot close to the building. Sometimes I see a few of them hanging out in the parking lot. They're either sitting in their cars smoking or, on nice days, standing near their vehicles. There is absolutely no smoking on our property. The landlord is crazy about that."

Ethan listened patiently, running his hand lightly across Molly's tummy. The dog lay squarely between the two of them.

"I remembered that there is a woman about my age and my size with dark hair. I'm not sure how long it is because she always wears it on top of her head under a baseball cap. I've talked to her a couple times. Small talk. 'Hi, how are you.' That kind of thing. Her name is Lauren."

"You must know her pretty well if you know her name."

"Not well, but I introduced myself once. And then she introduced herself."

"She probably appreciated you doing that. Most people simply ignore the cleaning crew."

"You're right. Anyway, I think she's a smoker. I hope she remembers that I'm a nice person because I'm going to ask her if I can use her badge and her baseball hat for a half hour."

"Really? And you think she'll be willing to do that?"

"I don't know. But what I do know is that I need a badge to get into the building. I have to have something to show the guard at the front desk. I'm counting on the fact that he'll see the baseball hat and won't look twice."

"Then what?"

"Once I'm in, I'm going to have to avoid the other workers. The guard and probably the supervisors can be fooled, but the coworkers who work with this woman every day are certainly going to know."

"So the plan is to somehow get this woman to let you use her identification, get past the guard and then make yourself scarce so that nobody sees you jump on a computer."

"Exactly."

He lightly sucked on the corner of his bottom lip, as if he were figuring out a way to tell her that her plan was so full of holes she should call it Swiss cheese.

"I know that you've talked to this woman before and I'm sure she thinks you're very nice but do you really think she's going to hand over her identification to you? No questions asked? And risk her job?"

"No. I think she'll be very reluctant. May tell me to go to hell."

"Isn't she going to want to know why you're not using your own badge?"

"I'm sure she will. I'm going to tell her I misplaced mine and that I'm afraid to tell my boss because I might get fired."

"That might get you some sympathy," Ethan said. "Especially from somebody who works for jerks."

"I'm also going to offer her an incentive. But I need you for that."

He raised an eyebrow.

She smiled. "Nothing indecent. I was just hoping that you'd let me borrow some more cash. I will pay you back, I promise."

"I'm not worried about that. How much are you thinking?"

"I'll start at five hundred."

He nodded. "It might work. She probably doesn't earn five hundred a week. Now all she has to do is hand over her ID for a half hour to someone she sort of knows, probably likes." He paused. "It's still a long shot."

"I know. But I don't think there's any other way inside. I have to have a badge. There's no way around it."

"What about a uniform? Does the cleaning crew wear them?" he asked.

She shook her head. "Once they are inside, everybody puts on a button-up blue smock."

"It sounds as if you've got your bases covered but I still don't like the fact that you'll be going in there by yourself. Whether it's Marcus White or your stepmother, they may be watching for you to try to access the property again. Because they haven't heard from the authorities, they have to assume that you haven't gone to them yet. If either one was responsible for the accident, he or she knows that your body wasn't found with the car. I suspect they are watching your condo and the office."

"Well, then I'm just going to have to get in and out fast, before they see me."

He shook his head. "Keep thinking. We need to find a way for me to get inside, too."

"I'm going to have to think fast. We're ten minutes away and the cleaning crew will start arriving soon after that. I only saw her vehicle once. It was a small SUV, white."

"Great. We'll be on the lookout for it, while at the same time keeping our eyes open for our friends in the light-colored car to resurface or our buddies in the black Suburban to show up again."

"This is getting complicated." Her brother was the one who liked to play cat-and-mouse games to outsmart the enemy. Mack had been into that since he'd been a little kid.

She, on the other hand, had liked to play math games on the computer when she was a young girl and now, as an adult, she felt pretty daring when she chose the intermediate slope on her ski trips.

She didn't court danger.

Yet in the past thirty hours, her car had been run off the side of a mountain, her cabin had been blown up, she was being pursued by at least one set of bad guys and now she was about to sneak into her place of employment so that she could get proof that somebody had committed treason.

It was unbelievable.

Almost as unbelievable as having sex with Ethan Moore. Maybe she didn't court danger, but she wasn't running from it, either.

WHEN ETHAN PULLED into the industrial park that housed Linder Automation, he realized that Chandler had omitted an interesting tidbit of information. The industrial park was built around a small private airport that had two nice runways, big enough for small planes to take off and land. "You never said anything about the airport."

She shrugged. "I'm sorry. I guess I don't even think about it anymore. Actually, this airport is how my dad met Claudia Linder."

"Sounds like an interesting story."

"I guess. Not one with a terribly happy ending." She gave him a soft smile. "At least from my perspective." She pointed her hand toward the rear of the park. "The airport was here first and then the industrial park came thirty years later. It's attractive to those business owners who have planes. That's how Claudia Linder ended up here. Her first husband had a plane and when he died, she decided to take flying lessons and keep his plane."

"How does that involve your dad?"

"My dad is still tinkering with his helicopters. He found this airport many years ago. He really likes it. There's no tower on-site, so it's mostly small planes and some helicopters that use it. What's really cool is that the hangars that they rent for helicopters have retractable roofs. Push a button and the roof folds up like an accordion. You can take off from inside the building. My dad loves that."

"I've seen a few of those over the years. They're handy."

"Yes. Dad had kept a helicopter here for several years when he got a good buy on a second helicopter. He needed another hangar. That's when he met Claudia Linder. She had a little Cessna in the one next door."

"I guess I always assumed that you had introduced them."

"Oh, no. Unfortunately, I didn't know about it right away. Maybe I could have prevented conversations over the wings from ending up being coffee in the cockpit and afternoon rides over the city."

"Romance bloomed on the tarmac?"

"I guess. Mack said something once about them starting their own mile-high club but I told him to shut up, that I really didn't need to carry that image around with me."

"Does your dad still keep his helicopters out here?"

"Just one now. Hangar 28. You can't see it from here. It's about a half mile to the north, near the edge of the industrial park." She turned her head to look at him. "Now that you're back, I'm sure he'd love to take you up. He's got an old Kiowa, one like he used to fly in Vietnam."

Ethan had known Baker flew Kiowas in the war. When it had come time to choose what he would fly, he could have chosen a Black Hawk or a Chinook or even been a hotdogger in one of the Apaches. He'd chosen the Kiowa and had loved every minute of it. Flying fast and low, sometimes barely above the tree line, he had gathered vitally important surveillance information and provided air support for ground troops.

There were many nights flying into enemy territory when he'd thought of Baker McCann and how the man had made similar missions over Vietnam. "That would be cool to go up with your dad," he said. "I'm sure he's busy, though."

"Not too busy for you, Ethan. You were like another son to him."

If only. He hadn't wasted much time thinking about how his life might have been different if he'd been the one born into the McCann family rather than Mack. But every once in a while, when he'd been in high school, and he'd gone to school all day and worked all evening at the grocery store so that he'd have some money to contribute to the household and a little of his own, he had wondered.

When he'd enlisted, he'd worked harder than almost anybody. And his efforts had been recognized. He'd gotten to do the type of work that he'd loved.

Until somebody had ripped the joy away.

He turned his head to look at her. "He already has a son. And a gorgeous daughter."

Chandler frowned at him, as though she sensed that something was wrong. "I'd be happy to show his helicopter to you sometime."

"I imagine your dad has the hangar locked up tight. It sounds as if this helicopter holds some real sentimental value to him."

"Of course, but there's a keypad. I know the combination." Chandler raised her arm and pointed at a six-story building toward the middle of the block. "That's Linder Automation," she said.

It was a rather nondescript office building. Redbrick. Glass front. Windows that didn't open. Flat roof with what was probably an air-conditioning unit on top. Right now it was just a big glob of snow.

There was a large parking lot directly to the north. There were only two vehicles in the lot. Both were empty. Neither was a black Suburban, a light-colored sedan or a small white SUV. "Recognize either of them?" he asked.

Chandler shook her head. "No. Occasionally people have to travel for work. They leave their vehicles here and take the train to the airport."

He figured she might be right. The lot had already been plowed but it appeared as if the plow had had to work around the two cars, and that had irritated the snowplow driver. Big drifts were piled behind the rear bumpers. If Denver didn't get a spring thaw in a couple days, the employees returning to these cars were in for a very unpleasant surprise. He hoped they had a shovel in their vehicles.

"I thought you said the supervisors get here a little earlier," Ethan said.

"They don't park outside. There's some limited underground parking that the executives use during the daytime. It's a big joke at work. If you're a vice president, you get an office with a window and a door opener for the underground parking garage. At night, the supervisors park their vehicles there. Like I said, they like to pretend that they are big shots on all levels."

Ethan didn't pull into the circular drive but he did

slow down slightly as he drove past. The lobby was lit up and there was a security guard sitting on a high stool behind a circular counter. He had a big round face and had lost most of his hair. He was reading the newspaper.

Ethan guessed the man's age at close to sixty. And he didn't look in great shape. "Is the security guard armed?" Ethan asked.

Chandler shook her head. "Nobody would trust Security Pete with a gun. I think he has pepper spray and a big flashlight."

"Security Pete?"

"That's how he always identifies himself. When he announces a visitor, he always says, 'This is Security Pete at the front desk.' Everybody in the building calls him Security Pete. Some of us," she said, smiling, "call him SSP, for Super Security Pete."

"I can tell you do government work—everything gets an acronym." Ethan kept driving, picking up his speed just a little. He hadn't been followed, he was confident of that. However, he didn't see any value in intentionally advertising his final destination.

Chandler had been confident that the man at the store was staring at Ethan. But what if he'd really been looking at Chandler and had simply averted his eyes when Chandler happened to look his direction? That could mean that the man had known Chandler and if so, he might also know where she worked. He wouldn't have needed to follow him and Chandler. He could have made a fairly safe bet and beat them to Linder Automation. It was possible that even right now he was watching for them.

Ethan wasn't going to take any chances.

He drove to the end of the block and turned left. Then with a series of successive turns, he ended up on one of the residential streets that faced the front entrance of Linder Automation. There were only two parking spots available and he parallel-parked the truck in one of them and cut his lights. They were too far away to see into the lobby but at the right angle to see the entrance of the employee parking lot. He twisted in his seat to look at her. "So, figured out a way to get me inside?"

"No."

He had. It had come to him when he'd seen the no-parking signs plastered every few feet, all the way around the semicircle drive in front of the building. "You said some of the workers come all together in a van."

"Yes. There's no public transportation out to this area. I suspect many of the workers don't have their own transportation and the cleaning company either goes to their individual houses and picks them up or more likely, picks them up at some central meeting point in the city that is accessible by the public transportation system."

"Where does the van go after it drops them off?"

She thought for a minute. "I have no idea. I mean, it has to be parked somewhere because the man driving the van also is one of the workers."

"I bet they park in the underground parking, where the supervisors park."

"Maybe. I'm not sure where this is going."

"You've been in this parking area, right?"

"Sure. After Claudia married my dad, they would occasionally ask me to meet them for dinner after work. We generally met somewhere near here because he'd be at the hangar. Claudia and I would ride together in her car and after dinner, one of them would bring me back so that I could pick up my car in the outside lot."

"So is there an elevator that takes the executives to the parking level?"

"Yes. Stairs, too, I believe, but we always took the elevator from the third floor, where Claudia's office is."

"Okay. Here's what we're going to do. When all the employees get out of the van, I'm going to get in."

"How are you going to do that? The driver stays in the vehicle. He'll see you."

"We need to give everyone something to focus on when they're getting out of the van."

She cocked her head. "Create some kind of disturbance?"

"Just a little one. Something to look at. There's a trash can outside the front door. I'm going to hide on the side of the building. When the van makes the corner, I'm going to throw a match into the trash and get a little fire going. Nothing too big, just something to get their attention. That may also help you because it will likely get the guard's attention, too, and he might not be checking IDs as closely as usual."

"The timing will have to be perfect."

"My life for the past twenty years has been flying helicopters in and out of combat zones. My timing is pretty good."

"This is different."

"Trust me."

"There's no question about that, Ethan. I trust you with my life."

His throat felt tight. "Good," he managed.

"Let's assume everything works up to that point. What happens once you're in the van?"

"I'll hide in the back. Once the van is parked inside

and the driver is out, I'll get on the elevator and you can meet me at the third floor."

"It seems like a ridiculous amount of effort just so that you can be inside with me. I'm going to be okay. I just have to find an office, log on, download the information from the server to my flash drive and get out. Besides, what are you going to do with Molly?"

"She can stay in the truck. I'll crack the window just a little bit. Fortunately the temperature has come up a little. She'll be fine."

"It's really not necessary," she insisted.

"I can't shake the feeling that it's dangerous for you to go into that building. I won't take the chance."

His words hung heavy in the air. Maybe it wasn't a declaration of love but it was definitely something. But as if by tacit agreement, Chandler wasn't asking for more specifics, and he didn't feel prepared to offer up anything.

Chandler McCann had gotten to him.

Big-time.

She deserved to know that people hated him. Her proximity to him might be putting her at risk as much as her own entanglements.

But he hadn't talked to anybody about what had happened overseas. He couldn't. Not even Chandler.

He was getting inside that building. If he couldn't be honest with her, he sure as hell was going to protect her.

Chapter Twelve

At twenty minutes after three, she saw an SUV come down the snow-covered street, the white vehicle almost blending into its surroundings. It made the right-hand turn into the lot and pulled into the empty third row.

"I think that's Lauren," she said. "Now or never."

Chandler had never felt so ill to her stomach.

"Wish me luck," she added.

Ethan didn't respond. He just grabbed her and kissed her hard.

She smiled at him. Now she'd have shaky legs, too, but it was worth it. She loved kissing him.

They each opened their door. Molly whined, as if she knew something was not right. Chandler reached back in and petted the dog on her head. "It'll be okay," she said, talking to the dog, hoping to reassure everyone.

"At least you've got boots now," Ethan muttered. He led the way down the snow-packed sidewalk. When they reached the end, he grabbed her hand and squeezed her fingers hard. "Be careful," he said.

She managed a nod, licked her lips and crossed the street at an angle that was out of the security guard's line of vision. She didn't think it mattered. The man rarely looked up from his newspaper.

It was definitely Lauren's car. Chandler's heart started to beat faster. When she knocked on the window, Lauren's head jerked up.

"Hi," Chandler said.

Lauren rolled down the window. She was smoking and she had her checkbook open in her lap, some unpaid bills next to her and a roll of stamps. As crazy as the night was, Chandler wanted to smile. She always paid her bills sitting in her car, too.

She felt bad for having scared the woman. It was the middle of the night in an empty parking lot. "It's me, Chandler McCann."

"Oh, hi," Lauren said. "It's pretty late for you to be working, isn't it?"

It was the perfect opening. "It is. I'm in trouble with my supervisor for not getting something done. He's being a jerk about it."

"They're all idiots. Make 'em a supervisor and suddenly they think they're God."

It was exactly the reaction she was hoping for. "Problem is, I forgot my ID badge so I can't get in the building."

"Can't you just tell the guard and he'll let you in?"

Chandler shook her head. "He's friends with my boss. I see them talking all the time. He'll tell him and then I'll be in trouble for not having my identification on me. You know what a stink that causes in a high-security building. I, uh, was hoping you might be able to help me."

"I could try," Lauren said as she looked at her watch.

"Can I borrow your badge and your baseball cap? I'm confident I can get past Security Pete at the desk. It won't take me long to get the work done and then I'll bring your stuff right back to you."

"I could get fired for giving my badge to someone else," Lauren said, sounding nervous.

"I know, I know. I wouldn't ask if I wasn't confident that I won't get you in any trouble." Now was the time to sweeten the deal. "I don't think you'll be able to work today because Security Pete might remember having already let you in the building once. You will need to call in sick to your company. But to compensate you for your time and trouble, I'm willing to give you five hundred dollars in cash."

The woman frowned at her. "Cash? Five hundred? And all I have to do is let you borrow my badge for a half hour?"

"Yes."

"You're not doing anything illegal, are you?"

"No way. You know that my stepmother, Claudia Linder McCann, is the CEO of Linder Automation. I'm not crazy about her but I would never do anything to hurt her or the company. My dad would never forgive me."

She'd read somewhere that the best liars were the ones who stuck closest to the truth.

It must have worked because Lauren was nodding. "Your stepmother won't even look at the cleaning crew. It's as if we're the dirt that we sweep up."

Out of the corner of her eye, Chandler saw another vehicle coming down the road. It was the cleaning crew van. She needed to be inside and through security before the rest of the workers got there.

She wanted to turn around to make sure that Ethan was safely out of sight, but she didn't want to call attention to him. If Lauren thought something weird was going on, she might get spooked.

"What do you say?" she asked, pulling the five hundred dollars out of her pocket.

Lauren looked at the money. Then she grabbed it out of Chandler's hand. "Here," she said, shoving the baseball cap toward Chandler. "Take my jacket, too. With that and the baseball cap, the security guard won't look at you twice. I'm getting out of here. I don't want those stupid supervisors seeing my car." She grabbed the envelope in her lap and ripped off the handwritten return address. "Here's my address. Just put my ID in my mailbox. I work in two days so I'll need it before then."

"Perfect," Chandler said, taking the scrap of paper.

Lauren started her car and pulled out of the lot. Chandler put Lauren's coat on over her own jacket and jammed the baseball hat on her head. She caught her long hair up in her hand, wound it tightly into a bun, and stuffed it up inside the hat, the way Lauren always wore hers. Both the hat and the coat smelled like smoke.

Her heart was hammering in her chest, making it hard to breathe. She walked briskly up the sidewalk and she could hear the engine of the van as it pulled into the circular drive.

She pulled on the door and Security Pete looked up.

And she felt his gaze linger.

And she knew that she'd horribly underestimated him.

She fought the urge to turn and run. She extended her badge, the way she'd seen the cleaning crew do, and willed her damn traitorous arm to stay steady.

He leaned forward.

And at just that minute, there was a commotion outside the window. She heard yelling but didn't turn her head to look.

Security Pete did. "Hells bells," he said. "Damn smokers."

And she knew the fire in the trash can had caught.

He pulled a fire extinguisher from under the counter and pushed his chair back. Two hundred and fifty pounds shifted.

Let me in. Push the button.

Security Pete ran his big fat hand across the sensor. The red bar lifted. She was in.

Game on.

ETHAN HAD USED his old newspapers to start the fire, wadding them up tight so that they didn't burn out too fast. He'd added them to the garbage container, which was already about half-full. Once he'd been sure the fire was going to take, he'd quickly hidden at the side of the building and watched the van approach.

The plan had gone even better than he'd hoped. Four people got out of the back of the van and when they noticed the smoke and started hollering, the driver of the van had scooted across the bench seat and gotten out on the passenger side to see what the fuss was all about.

That had given Ethan the chance to move out of the shadows, cross in front of the van's headlights, move alongside the van and slip inside the open back door into a dark corner. After a minute, somebody shut the back door. The driver got back inside, never realizing that he'd picked up a passenger.

Ethan could tell when they pulled into the underground parking area because there was more light coming into the van. That meant more opportunity for discovery. He didn't want to hurt the driver, but there was no way he was going to let the man alert others and potentially cause problems for Chandler.

It drove him crazy that she was out of his sight. She had proven time and again that she was tougher than she looked, but the idea of her getting harmed in any way made him want to punch something. Instead, he braced himself to take the curves as the van lumbered along. The best thing he could do to help Chandler was to get inside without incident.

The van slowed, made a sharp right-hand turn and then stopped. The driver killed the ignition.

Now it was absolutely still inside the vehicle. Ethan forced himself to breath naturally, quietly, and after a few seconds of what sounded like the man fumbling with his seat belt, the door on the driver's side opened.

The door closed. Ethan heard the man's footsteps fade as he walked away. Ethan raised his head, just high enough to see the man swipe what appeared to be a plastic card in some kind of electronic badge reader. Then he pulled on the heavy metal door. It opened. Ethan saw the stairs that Chandler had mentioned. The man went inside and the door swung shut behind him.

Chandler hadn't mentioned that the door required a badge swipe. She probably didn't know. She had said that she and her stepmother left from work to meet Baker but she'd probably never arrived at work through the garage.

Ethan got out of the van, closing the door as softly as he could. He hurried toward the elevator, with every step feeling the heavy weight of the handgun that he carried in his jacket pocket.

He pushed the up button on the elevator. It blinked but

didn't stay on. The doors remained closed. He pushed it again. Same results.

And then he saw it. There was a badge reader next to the elevator.

Damn it.

The reality of his situation hit him. Both the stairs and the elevator required a badge to enter. It was no doubt different once you were inside the building. Then, employees could use both in traveling from floor to floor and when exiting.

He was trapped in the parking garage.

Chandler was on her own.

CHANDLER HAD AN office on the fourth floor. She did not head for it. Instead, she went to the third floor and waited for Ethan as planned.

The exterior walls were lined with offices on three sides and a big conference room on the fourth side. All the doors were closed. The interior space was filled with groups of cubicles, with high padded walls designed to absorb the sounds of busy workers. But it was all quiet now, with just a few lights dimly lit.

She waited for the ding of the elevator, to let her know that Ethan was near.

But the only noise she heard in the room was the motor on the water cooler that sat along the wall, halfway between the elevator and the stairs.

The closest bay of cubicles was where the marketing staff worked. She sat down at one of the computers, turned it on, signed in with her test user account and watched both the elevator and the blinking computer cursor.

Where the hell was Ethan?

Had he been discovered by the van driver?

Her stomach twisted in fear.

She had no idea how long she might have before the cleaning crew got their vacuums and mops and made their way to the third floor. Lights would go on and she would be discovered.

She had to be out of there before that happened.

Her test user sign-on worked. She clicked through the screens, accessing the directory of server files. She scanned the list. What the hell had she named the file? She'd wanted something that wouldn't be obvious to somebody else that it was wedding information. She'd written the name down and put it under the telephone on her desk but she sure as hell couldn't go get it now.

Wait, there it was. *Binding Intent.*

She inserted the flash drive that she'd purchased at the store and watched the screen to make sure the downloading process was working. Her heart was thumping in her chest. It was a big file and it seemed to be taking forever.

Please, please let Ethan be okay, she silently prayed.

Forty percent downloaded. Sixty-five percent. Eighty-three percent. She watched the messages on her screen. Almost done.

She heard a noise outside the door. If she jerked the flash drive out before the file was completely down-loaded, she risked ruining the data.

Ninety-two percent.

A door across the room was opening.

One hundred percent.

She clicked the mouse, exited the program, pulled the flash drive and ran for the elevator. She pushed the button.

"Stop," someone ordered. "Security."

She turned, ready to show him her—Lauren's—ID badge. A man, all in black, his arms extended, stood in the doorway. He was holding a deadly-looking gun that was pointed at her.

Pulling a weapon wasn't normal protocol under these circumstances. Clearly the security guard had been given orders to use force if necessary.

Which meant her ID badge was going to be useless in this situation.

She made a move to go right toward the stairs, then heard the soft ding of the elevator. She quickly reversed and threw herself into the elevator when the doors opened.

She slammed her hand on the close button.

The gun went off, and she heard a terrible noise as his shot hit the closed elevator door. She wanted to sag to the floor in relief.

But she stayed on her damn feet.

This wasn't over.

When the door opened at the basement level, she took off running, knowing that she had only a few seconds' lead on the strange man and his gun.

She almost had a heart attack when a dark shape emerged from the shadows. "No," she squeaked.

"It's me," Ethan said. "What happened?"

"They saw me and—"

She didn't have to explain because at that exact moment the stairway door burst open and the man stepped out and started shooting at them.

Ethan pushed her out of the way, behind one of the big concrete columns that supported the structure. He followed her and got behind cover just as a bullet hit the concrete, sending bits of debris flying.

"Get in the van," he ordered. "Keys are in the ignition. Get the hell out of here. Do it now." He moved, leaving his protection, and returned fire.

She wanted to yank him back, to keep him safe. Instead, she ran for the van, knowing that he was right.

She could hear the exchange of gunfire as she ripped open the driver's-side door. She turned the key in the ignition. All she had to do was put the vehicle in Drive and get the hell out.

She put the van in Reverse, backed up fast and almost hit Ethan. The gunman, realizing what she was doing, had switched tactics and was now firing at the van. One of the back windows exploded.

Ethan jumped in the passenger side. "Get down!"

It was going to be hard to do that and drive.

But she tried.

She gunned the motor while Ethan pushed the button on the visor to raise the big garage door. She cleared the entranceway and hit the steep snow-covered incline going too fast. The vehicle fishtailed, almost knocking into the concrete sidewalls.

She somehow managed to maintain control and they were on the street.

"Don't stop now, honey," Ethan urged. He had closed the garage door behind them just as soon as they'd cleared it but they both knew that it was likely the guard wasn't going to give up so easily.

She took the time to spare him a glance. He had a thin line of blood running down his face where he'd been hit with flying concrete. Other than that, he was whole.

And so was she.

It had never been so wonderful to be alive.

And then she heard the thump-thump of a tire going flat. "Tire," she said, holding the wheel firmly.

Ethan rolled down his window and stuck his head out. "Right rear. Keep driving," he instructed. "Get us as close to the airfield as you can."

"What?"

"We've got to get out of here. Fast. Getting back to my truck is too risky. We need another way."

"What are you going to do?"

He shrugged. "You said that you could get into your dad's hangar. I hope you're right because I think that's our best way out of here. We're going to fly out."

The van limped along to hangar 28. They got out and ran for the door. Ethan had his gun out, ready to shoot, while Chandler punched the numbers in. There were two sets of headlights coming down the street. Fast.

Ethan heard a click and the big door went up. They ducked under as soon as there was enough space.

The helicopter was beautiful.

"Can you fly this?" Chandler asked.

He could fly most anything. But could they get the beast started and out of there before they had company?

Chapter Thirteen

Ethan's hands were a blur of motion as he flipped switches and did all the things necessary to get her dad's pride and joy into the air. Having watched her father a few times, Chandler had a rudimentary knowledge of what he was doing but certainly could not have been any help.

He didn't need any. That was clear. The minute he'd stepped into the helicopter, she'd felt the change in him. He was calm, totally in the moment, totally focused.

She knew enough to put her headset on and to strap in. The engine was going, the blades were rotating. The roof was wide open. Ethan turned to her and gave her a brilliant smile and a thumbs-up.

And suddenly they were in the air, clearing the building, lifting. She gripped her seat, expecting to feel gunfire hit the frame of the helicopter. The security guard had been crazy enough to try to shoot her inside the building. What was going to stop him from firing off a few rounds now?

She looked down. There was a light-colored SUV parked next to the building, a man standing next to it, his arm raised in the air.

She waited.

But Ethan was moving fast, doing a little bit of a bob and weave that would have made it difficult for even the most experienced of shooters. And it made her stomach tight to think that he'd lived a life where this was second nature, to make it very hard for the enemy to hit your aircraft.

It took only seconds for them to be out of range. It seemed as if it was an eternity. She could no longer see the man. The sky was dark and the city off to their south was a blur of lights.

She had no idea where they were headed but still, Chandler felt her chest relax for the first time since she'd approached Lauren in the car. "That was close," she said, grateful for the small microphones attached to the headset. She needed to talk, to express her pent-up emotion. "Too close."

"Are you okay?" he asked.

"I am now."

"I'm sorry that I couldn't get inside," he said. "The elevator was locked. I needed a card swipe."

She nodded. "I knew something had gone wrong. I was able to log on and I started downloading the file I needed. I was just finishing when the guy showed up. We never have armed security in the building. And he didn't even hesitate to start shooting. I think he was watching for me."

"Now what?"

"I'm going to look at what's in the file. If the evidence is there, I'm going to the FBI."

"Even if it proves that your stepmother did this?"

"Even then. I'm tired of people trying to kill me, Ethan. Now they're trying to kill you, too. It's gone too far."

"What do you need in order to look at the file?"

"Just a computer. Mine, unfortunately, was in my backpack and we both know that story. I have an old desktop at my apartment but I'm not sure it would be safe to go there."

"I doubt it. There's a guy that I served with who lives in Denver. We were pretty close friends. I could call him and see if we could use his computer, since there isn't a place open where we can access computers by the hour."

"We're just going to…uh…drop in and park in his backyard?" she asked, waving her hand around.

He turned his head and smiled at her. "There's an elephant in the room and we're in it."

As always, she really appreciated his sense of humor. "Hard to arrive quietly in this," she said.

"You're right. Also, we have the small problem of my truck being parked near Linder with Molly in it." He looked at his watch. "It's almost four. It won't be light for another two hours. We need to use that to our advantage."

"I'm sure they're searching the area right now. They may find your truck. I imagine they have the means to run the plates. That, combined with any security footage they have from the basement parking area, may be enough. People are going to realize that you're with me. I'm so sorry, Ethan, for dragging you into this."

"I'm not worried," he said. "They are going to have to check every vehicle on several different streets. Even if they run my plates, there's nothing to connect the two of us."

She wasn't convinced. "When we get back on the ground, I *am* calling Mack. Claudia is involved. I know it. She's up to her neck in this. He needs to know."

"He's going to be thrilled that you're okay. Not knowing when we'd have access to a phone, I tried to get him that message."

"I don't understand."

"Your dad would have contacted Mack right away and he'd have come home fast. If he goes to the Donovan cabin, which I'm counting on, he'll know you're with me."

"He'll know this because…" She allowed her voice to trail off.

"I left him a note of sorts. Even when we were kids, your brother was always planning some sort of covert action. And he developed a way for the three of us to communicate. It's not perfect but it usually got the job done."

She processed what he said and it hit her. "The books. When we were leaving, you put Larry Donovan's book back on the shelf. And then you took the time to rearrange some. But you put them back upside down."

He nodded. "Upside down, at the end of every shelf."

"So how does it work?"

"You always use the first letter in the title. If you're missing a letter or you need a space, the upside-down book goes in the middle of the shelf, rather than at the end."

"What was your message?"

"CM with EM."

Chandler McMann with Ethan Moore. "Very smart," she said.

"Honey, if Claudia is behind all this, the security company has contacted her and she knows."

"Then we need to bring this to an end. Quickly." She could feel him shift the direction of the helicopter. "Where are we going?" she asked.

"Look down there. Looks like one of those multiscreen movie theatres. Don't really care what the business is just as long as the parking lot is big and there are no low-hanging wires in the way. We're going to park this thing."

"How far away are we from Linder?"

"Far enough. I suspect about five miles away as the crow flies."

"Are we walking back to the truck?"

He smiled. "I sure as hell hope not. This city has cabs, right?"

She wasn't confident how much luck they'd have snagging a cab at four in the morning. "There's a bus that stops four blocks from Linder. I took it to work a few mornings when my car was in the shop."

"That will work, too. Hang on."

She didn't need to hang on. He landed the helicopter so deftly, it was as if they were a cotton ball falling from the sky. She'd spent some time in helicopters over the years due to her father's obsession and she'd never had a better landing. "You're really good," she said.

"I loved flying," he said simply. "Loved teaching others how to do it, as well."

Once again, there was something there, something in the tone of his voice, the look in his eye. "But yet you quit? I wonder about that. Did something happen to you when you were serving?"

He didn't answer. Instead, he shut down the helicopter, each flip of a switch very deliberate, very exact. Once the blades stopped turning, he turned to her. "We should get going," he said, absolutely no emotion in his voice.

She wanted to demand that he tell her but she didn't. It hurt that he didn't trust her, or even worse, didn't care enough to share something that had clearly been important to him.

She wasn't going to beg. They'd been as close as two people could physically be but yet he seemed determined to hold her at arm's length, to keep her outside of Ethan Moore's private thoughts.

They'd had a few hours of great sex. Maybe that's all it ever could be. And five years from now, when some woman finally corralled her brother into marriage, they'd both be at the wedding. They'd have polite conversation, the kind seen at class reunions, where attendees had a shared childhood but not much else in common.

It sounded horrible.

She got out of the helicopter and stood in the dark parking lot, feeling empty and tired. She pulled the cell phone out of her pocket and punched in Mack's number. It rang four times before going to voice mail. "Mack McCann." When she heard her brother's voice, she wanted to weep. Instead she took a deep breath and waited for the beep. "Mack, it's Chandler. I'm…I'm okay. I'm with Ethan Moore. And we need to talk to you. Don't tell anyone that I called. Not even Dad, okay? Call me back on this number. I love you."

She pressed the disconnect button. "Well, that's that."

"He'll call as soon as he gets the message. He may be in an airplane somewhere. For now, let's just focus on getting back to the truck."

It took her a minute to get her bearings but when she did, she realized that she'd been to the movie theater before. It had been a couple years. She'd met friends who lived in another part of Denver.

"I know where we are," she said. "Well, sort of. That highway leads back into the heart of the city. They built this theater about five years ago. Land is a lot less expensive out here."

"How far of a walk?"

"We'll be back in civilization within a mile or so." *Then we can finish this thing and you can be on your way.* She managed to keep that thought to herself.

She wasn't surprised when he started walking fast.

ONCE THEY REACHED the main highway, there was some early-morning traffic. No one seemed to be paying much attention to them, not even the cab that Ethan tried to flag down to no avail.

"Sorry," Ethan muttered.

Chandler didn't answer. Ethan hadn't expected her to. She hadn't said a word since they'd walked away from the helicopter. It was his fault. She'd asked about his time in the service and he'd closed up fast.

He needed to tell her the truth.

He would. Just as soon as this whole thing was over.

He saw another cab and raised his arm. It was a risk to get a ride but every minute that went by, there was an even greater risk that his truck would be discovered or that evidence would be destroyed. The cab slowed. The driver looked at them, apparently judged them to be fairly nonthreatening and therefore ride-worthy, and stopped. Ethan opened the door and Chandler stepped inside and scooted across the seat.

She was practically hugging the other door.

He tried to tell himself that a little distance between the two of them might be good. After all, they'd met and been in bed together in less than twenty-four hours. Maybe a little distance would aid perspective.

"Where to?" the cab driver asked.

Ethan gave him the major cross streets that were about four blocks away from Linder Automation. The man nodded, flipped on his meter and took off fast.

It was about a ten-minute ride. When they got to the busy intersection, Ethan could see that the city was coming to life. There were garbage trucks rumbling up and down the snow-covered streets and even an occasional pedestrian bundled up in a coat, scarf and boots.

Ethan handed the fare to the driver and opened the door. He waited until the car had driven off before turning to Chandler. "I figured this was close enough. We'll walk the rest of the way. I'm hoping that we can approach quietly, get in the truck and be out of there before anybody notices." He studied her. "We should have bought you a warmer coat at the store."

She waved a hand. She still had Lauren's red coat over her own denim jacket. "I'm fine," she said. "Let's go. I want to see what's on this flash drive."

While the snowfall in Denver had not been as significant as it had been in the mountains, there were many spots where the sidewalk hadn't yet been shoveled. And people who had shoveled were going to be disappointed because the wind was whipping the snow around, undoing much of their hard work. They had a choice to walk through drifts that came up to their knees or walk in the street. They chose the street. Ethan kept Chandler in front of him and they walked single file.

She slipped once on the icy street and he caught her before she could fall. Once she was in his arms, he turned her so that he could see her face.

"Thanks," she said, her voice high.

The early morning wind sent several strands of her

beautiful silky hair across her pink cheeks. Her green eyes were bright and so very alive. She was simply stunning.

And he couldn't resist her.

At dawn, under the streetlights, standing at the edge of a snow-covered highway, he framed her face with his hands and kissed her.

And when she responded and he felt her energy enter his body and warm it, it seemed as if everything was right in the world.

Screw distance. Screw perspective.

He wasn't sure when it had hit him—he thought perhaps when he'd seen her exit the elevator in the basement at a run and then realized that someone was shooting at her—that he loved her.

And he didn't intend to let her go.

He wanted to proclaim his love, wanted her to know it, wanted the world to know it. But when he pulled back, he kept his mouth shut. It wasn't even the right time to be kissing her. It certainly wasn't the right time or place to be telling her that he wanted to have a future with her. He didn't have a job or a real place to live. That might have been how his stepfather did business, not having a clue how he was going to provide for his family, but it wasn't how Ethan intended to do it.

"Ethan?" she asked, confusion in her eyes.

He ran the pad of his thumb across her lips. "Later," he promised. "We have things to do now." He turned her around and gave her a gentle push forward.

When they got to the block where his truck was parked, he stopped her. "Stay here," he said. "I'll get my truck and circle back for you. If I'm not back in five minutes, get the hell out of here. Use your phone. Call your dad. Call Mack. Call the police."

"I want to go with you," she said.

He shook his head. "You should get out of the wind. You could stand in that doorway," he said, pointing toward the all-glass front door of a brick building that had a narrow front but long sides that extended at least a hundred yards. On the door, yellow letters were stenciled. Homewood Plastics Fabrication. The front lobby area was still dark.

"I'll be back. Don't worry," he added. Then he brushed a kiss across her lips.

How could she not worry? Chandler stood under the green awning in the small doorway and watched the man she loved walk away. Her lips still tingled from his kiss. She could still feel his hands as they gripped her arms. Holding. Protecting. Cherishing.

She couldn't be misreading it, could she? She'd done that once before, with Christivo. Had badly misread the situation. But Ethan was no Christivo. He was honest and good and very worthy of love.

She hated being separated from him but she couldn't fault his logic. Each step closer to Linder, she became a bigger target.

On the walk back, she'd been reflecting upon what had happened inside Linder. It would have been reasonable if the security officer had said something like, "Hey, you, what are you doing in here?" But he hadn't. He'd barely even instructed her to stop before he'd tried to use deadly force to permanently stop her.

He hadn't called her by name, but he hadn't seemed all

that surprised to see her. It was as if he'd been coached to expect a young woman. That, more than anything, had convinced her that it was Claudia Linder who was behind the data theft and not Marcus White. Claudia had the resources and the authority to contract with some goons to provide security, to tell them to shoot first and ask questions later.

Chandler watched as Ethan turned the corner. Within seconds, he was out of her sight. She glanced at her watch. He had four minutes left.

Please, please let him be all right. Please let him be able to walk up to his truck, get in and drive away without incident. Please don't let me hear gunshots.

So intent was she on listening, she was absolutely unprepared when she felt the cold, hard pressure of a gun pressed up against the side of her neck.

She shrieked and was immediately yanked back by an arm around her neck. A man, much bigger and stronger than she was, pushed her up against the glass door.

"Shut up," he ordered.

He had on a face mask. All she could see was his dark brown eyes and his lips. He had a gray mustache.

"What do you want?" she asked.

"You're that woman," he said. "The one with her picture on the news. Said you were missing."

Chandler's heart sank. "You've got me confused with somebody. I'm just waiting for the bus."

"Don't lie to me, lady. I saw you with him. I saw you with that bastard Ethan Moore. I tried to follow you. When I lost you, I was so angry. Then I remembered that the news had said where you worked."

So it was the man she saw looking at Ethan at the store earlier!

"What do you want with Ethan?" she asked.

"Fortunately, your office wasn't that hard to find. I got here just in time to see the son of a bitch take off in the helicopter. I knew it was him."

"I don't understand," Chandler said. Ethan would be back any minute. She had to find a way to talk some sense into this man before he arrived. "How do you know Ethan?"

His eyes narrowed. "I don't know him. I don't want to know him. He's scum. A traitor. They should cut his head off and put it on a pole like they do in those god-forsaken countries that we keep trying to save."

None of that made sense. Ethan loved his country, had risked his life on almost a daily basis to protect it. *A traitor?* Not possible. "Ethan is a good—"

"My brother is dead because of him. My little brother," the man said, his voice breaking a bit. "He'd just gotten married the year before. Now his wife has no-body and she cries every day. Moore has to pay for that."

She could hear the man's genuine anguish in his voice. "There must be some mistake," Chandler said.

He grabbed her arm hard, wrenching her sore shoulder. She wanted to cry out but held it in. She didn't want him to know that she had any weaknesses.

He moved her so that his back was up against the glass door and she was directly in front of him. They were in the doorway, unable to be seen unless someone pulled up in front of the building.

"What are you going to do?" she asked.

"You'll see," he said. "When he comes to pick you up, you'll both see."

ETHAN APPROACHED HIS truck warily. He kept one hand in his pocket, where he carried his loaded gun. There were still lots of parked vehicles on the street.

He looked at the snow around the vehicle. He could see footprints. His. Chandler's. But nothing else. That reassured him somewhat. There'd certainly been time for somebody who knew what they were doing to plant an explosive device. But he didn't see any evidence of that.

He opened the door and woke Molly up. She licked his face and wanted to sit on his lap. He gave her a fast rub on the head. "Not now, girl. We've got things to do."

He started the engine, then looked at his watch. He'd been gone for three and a half minutes. That meant he had ninety seconds before Chandler took off.

He wasted no time in pulling away from the curb. He did a U-turn in the intersection and headed back the way he'd come. As he approached the place where he'd left Chandler, he got worried when he couldn't see her.

Then, as he pulled up in front of Homewood Plastics, his heart almost stopped. He could see Chandler, her face very white in comparison to Lauren's red coat. There was a man in a ski mask holding her in place, with his arm around her neck. In his other hand was a black gun that was pointed at Chandler's temple.

Chapter Fourteen

Ethan was a fighter pilot, trained to quickly examine and discard options until settling upon the optimum solution. But right now, all he could think of was that he was about to lose Chandler.

He rolled down his window and waited for the man to say something.

"Hello, Moore. I've been getting acquainted with your girlfriend."

The bastard knew his name. *Getting acquainted?* Did he not know Chandler? *Girlfriend?*

"What do you want?" Ethan asked. His throat felt dry and tight and he wondered how he could get a word out.

The man didn't answer but Chandler's head jerked back from where he'd tightened his hold on her. Ethan fought the urge to jump from the damn truck and rip the stranger to shreds. One bad move on his part and Chandler would be dead.

"Park your truck there and get out," the man ordered.

Ethan pulled into a space and killed the ignition. He opened the door and stepped out quickly before Molly could follow. The gun in his right coat pocket felt heavy. In his left pocket, the garage door opener to Linder

Automation that he'd pulled from the van before ditching it, much lighter.

Unbalanced.

He stood. Perfectly still. Breathing deep. Getting his head in the game.

"Come here," the man said.

Slowly, he started to walk toward them.

"That's far enough," the man said, stopping him after just a few steps. "We're going to take a ride in that Buick."

"I've got my dog," Ethan said, stalling for time.

"I can see that. I don't care." The man tossed him a set of keys. "You're going to drive."

Ethan raised his hand and caught the keys. He made eye contact with Chandler. *Don't worry. We'll be okay.*

She gave him an almost imperceptible nod. He got the message. *I trust you.*

Ethan's heart filled with resolve and his senses, always acute, edged up a notch. He would find his opportunity.

Ethan walked over to the car, stood by the driver's-side door and realized the light-colored sedan was likely the car that had followed them from the store's parking lot. It seemed as if Chandler had been right about the man being interested in Ethan.

In the console between the two front seats was a plastic employee badge. There was a logo for a company but no company name. The man's picture was on the badge. It had to be the same guy. The mustache was the same.

There was a first name and last initial and a job title on the badge. Ted M. CNC Machinist.

The prominence of the badge clearly suggested this wasn't a well-planned kidnapping—no one wearing a mask to hide his identity would intentionally leave a photo ID in the front of his car.

"It would be helpful if you told me what you wanted," Ethan said, trying to keep his tone conversational.

The man snorted. "I want justice."

A shiver ran up Ethan's spine. "For?"

"Shut up. Get in the car. Put both hands on the steering wheel where I can see them."

Ethan did as instructed. Once his hands were on the wheel, the man, using Chandler as a human shield, approached the car from the rear and got into the backseat.

In the rearview mirror, Ethan could see that the man now had one arm wrapped around Chandler's shoulder. His other arm was crossed over his body so that his gun rested against Chandler's ribs, pointing slightly up.

The bullet would go directly into her heart.

"Drive. Go back to the highway. Turn left."

Ethan put the car in gear and started forward. Out of the corner of his eye, he could see motion in the backseat. He turned his head, just enough to see. The man had a cell phone in the hand that was wrapped around Chandler's shoulder. He was texting something.

What the hell?

Ethan looked at the clock in the car. Almost five-thirty. It was still dark but the city was starting to come alive. There was more traffic than there had been a little more than two hours earlier when he and Chandler had first driven toward Linder Automation.

Ethan kept his eyes moving, looking for some local police presence. He could get their attention, give them some reason to stop the car.

But before he could do anything, the man leaned forward. His breath was hot on Ethan's neck. "Turn at the next street. There will be a yellow ranch, three houses in on the right. Hit the garage door opener on the dash. Pull in. Don't do anything stupid or she dies."

He saw the house. A one-car garage was attached. The yellow paint looked pretty fresh, the sidewalk had been shoveled and there was a fall wreath on the front door. Not exactly the place where he'd expect a killer to hang out.

"Shut the car off and close the door. Then get out. Put your hands on the hood where I can see them."

Ethan did exactly what he was told.

The light had come on in the garage when he'd pulled in and he hoped it would only stay on for a short while. Then the small space would be dark.

Perhaps that would give him the opportunity he needed.

He was counting the seconds in his head when he heard the man's cell phone ring. The guy answered it, spoke briefly and then shifted so that he could reach over the middle of the seat to again hit the garage door button and open the door.

A man, about sixty, with gray hair and weathered skin, wearing old jeans and a heavy coat, joined them in the garage. He had a troubled look on his face.

He stared at Ethan but didn't say a word. He pushed a button on the wall and the heavy garage door came down one more time.

The man in the backseat got out, dragging Chandler with him. The older man didn't even look at Chandler. In fact, it appeared that he was almost trying not to look at her.

The man with the gun pulled off his mask, and Ethan

noted every detail in case he had to identify him from a lineup later.

Assuming he and Chandler got out alive.

"Help me get him tied up, Dad."

"Damn it, Teddy, this is a hell of a mess," the older man said.

"It's for Trevor, Dad. We owe it to him."

Trevor.

It suddenly made sense. Private First Class Trevor Matchmore. Ethan had memorized all the names of the men who had been killed that night.

The brave soldier had been Ted's brother, most likely. The older man's son.

This trouble had nothing to do with Chandler. It was all about him. *I'm sorry, Chandler. So sorry.*

Did she understand what was happening? It almost seemed as if she did. Maybe Ted had told her something in those few minutes that he'd had while Ethan was retrieving his truck.

"Search him, Dad."

Ethan judged his options. Dad was in decent shape but certainly no match for him. But Ted still had the damn gun pointed at Chandler.

So he stood still, let Dad search him and made sure there was no change of expression when the man discovered the gun in his coat pocket.

Dad took the gun and the garage opener for Linder Automation and put them on a shelf in the garage. Then he turned Ethan around and pushed him toward the door that led into the house. Ethan went into a small kitchen that was currently being remodeled. Countertop had been removed. Everything between the old sink, which had probably been there since the house was built forty years ago, all the way to the stove in the corner was gone, leaving the cupboards below open to view. Ethan could see pots and pans and other kitchen things on the shelves.

There was a stack of newspapers on the table, with just one dirty plate and a coffee cup sitting next to it. The paper was open to an advertisement.

It was pretty clear what had happened. Maybe Ted worked second shift at some factory and had gotten home after work and had a snack. He'd been reading the paper, saw something in the ad that caught his eye and decided to make an early-morning run to the store. Maybe something he needed to finish his remodeling job.

There were probably only a handful of people who actually read a newspaper anymore. Just his luck, it was him and a crazy guy determined to avenge his brother's death.

Dad pushed down on Ethan's shoulder and Ethan sat in one of the straight-backed wooden chairs. Ted opened a drawer, grabbed some duct tape and tossed it to Dad. The man tore some off and motioned for Ethan to put his arms behind his back with his wrists together.

He obliged, keeping them positioned exactly right. Every soldier had been trained in maneuvers to escape enemy capture and there was a way to keep the restraints as loose as possible. Duct tape was one of the worst but it could be done.

Then Dad taped an ankle to each chair leg. He never said a word to Ethan, never looked him in the eye, not even when he slapped a piece of duct tape over his mouth.

When Dad was finished and Ted no longer considered Ethan a threat, he finally took his gun away from

Chandler. He put it down on the table and then roughly searched Chandler for weapons.

Ethan wanted to beat the hell out of him for touching her, for running his hands across her body. But Chandler showed no emotion. When the man found the flash drive and cell phone in Chandler's coat pocket, he held them up.

"What's this?" he asked.

"Work," she said, as if it was no great significance.

Ted tossed it into the middle of the kitchen table. He examined the cell phone and pushed a couple buttons. "Only one call. Practically brand-new."

"I lost my other one," Chandler supplied.

"For every piece of good luck I'm having, it appears you're having just as bad. Go figure." Then he pushed Chandler into a chair and he repeated Dad's actions, tying her up tight and covering her mouth with tape.

Ethan knew the position of her shoulder had to be causing her pain, but again, her face showed no indication. It was as if she were a well-trained soldier. Be compliant when appropriate, don't let the enemy know what's important to you, don't let the enemy know your areas of weakness, wait for your opportunity.

The trick of it all was not waiting too long.

Dad and Ted both took off their winter jackets and threw them on one of the empty kitchen chairs. Then they left the kitchen.

Ethan made eye contact with Chandler. He could see that she was trying to move her lips under the duct tape.

She was trying to smile.

Good girl. Stay calm. Keep thinking.

Ethan strained to hear the conversation in the other room. The men were talking in very low tones but he could still pick up bits and pieces of the conversation, mostly from Dad, whose voice carried better.

"Hell of a mess, Teddy," he said once again.

There was a reply that Ethan couldn't catch.

Then Dad was talking again. "I suppose that… work….think this through. I've…map in my car."

Ethan heard a door open and close and he assumed the father had gone outside to get the map. He heard an interior door close and then the soft sound of someone urinating.

He turned his wrists this way and that, slowly loosening the bind of the tape. Chandler watched him and he could see that she was doing the same. Duct tape was a very effective restraint. Fortunately Dad wasn't an expert in securing someone and his mind had probably been less on tying Ethan up and more on what the hell they were going to do with him.

He had made some progress in loosening the tape when he heard the front door open and close, then the sounds of a map being unfolded. After several minutes, there was discussion, too quiet for him to distinguish any words. Then the two men were back in the kitchen. Dad had the map in one hand; Ted had his gun.

After putting the gun down on the counter, Ted got scissors out of the drawer. He cut the tape off Chandler's ankles, freeing her legs. He did not take the duct tape off her mouth, nor did he free her arms. Instead he had her stand. Once again, he picked up his gun and pointed it at her. He motioned for Dad to cut Ethan free. Dad followed Ted's lead and freed both legs. Then he motioned for Ethan to stand.

Once Ethan was up with his hands still bound behind his back, Ted pushed Chandler toward the door.

She resisted, her eyes on the flash drive in the middle of the table.

"You're not going to need it," Ted said, his voice high.

Ethan didn't know if it was tension or excitement making the man's voice change. All he knew was that the men didn't intend for him and Chandler to be around for long. They were going to take them somewhere, probably remote, kill them and dump the bodies.

It wasn't the best plan for killing someone. Transporting them meant that there would be evidence left behind in their vehicles. Lots of DNA. But Ethan was pretty confident that it was the best plan the two men could come up with on short notice. This was a crime of opportunity. Ted had stumbled upon them in the store and he'd been making up the plan as he went along.

Ethan wasn't getting into the car with them and he sure as hell wasn't letting them take Chandler.

Ted handed his father the gun. "Don't take it off her." Then the younger man put on his coat and patted his pockets, looking for gloves.

Dad was focused on Chandler. When he went to hand the gun back to his son, Ethan made his move.

From his standing position, he crouched at the knees, then stood up fast, catching the exposed sharp edge of the old sink just right. He felt the duct tape give way.

His first punch caught Ted, his second Dad. Adrenaline whipped through his body as if he were seventeen again, fighting a man who was bigger and meaner.

Dad never got up. He stayed down, almost as if he were looking for an excuse for the whole mess to be over with. Ted scrambled up and Ethan executed another punch to take him down to his knees. Ethan kicked him in the stomach, hard enough to knock the man's breath out of him, but not hard enough to do damage.

It took him only seconds to subdue them both. He picked up the gun that had fallen on the floor. He held it on them with one hand while he used the scissors to cut the duct tape off Chandler's wrists. She pulled the duct tape off her mouth, then she pulled the tape off his mouth.

"Are you okay?" he asked.

"Yes. Thank you." She looked at Ted. "How's that luck going for you now?"

It was enough to make Ethan, who felt miserable about the situation she'd been dragged into, want to smile. The woman had spunk.

"This is my fault," he said.

"It's not," she replied simply. "We can talk about it later. What are we going to do with them?"

He had no idea. All he knew was that these were probably not bad men. They'd lost someone very dear to them, and grief and anger and family loyalty had made them do a crazy thing.

They needed to contact the police. But he knew that Chandler wanted to see what was on the flash drive first before confronting her stepmother.

"Do you have a computer?" Ethan asked Ted.

Ted nodded. It clearly wasn't the question he'd been expecting.

"Where?"

"In my bedroom."

Ethan looked at Chandler. "I'm going to tie these two up." He handed the gun to her. "If they move, shoot them."

Ethan used the same duct tape and the same chairs to

tie up Dad and Ted. He had learned how to effectively restrain a man in the military and there was no way those two were getting free. When he was finished, he reached for the flash drive and held it out to Chandler, exchanging it for the gun.

"Use his computer. See if you can read the file."

Chapter Fifteen

Ted's computer was a couple years old but he'd updated the software. She had no trouble opening the file. No trouble seeing the data. No trouble identifying which user had made screen print after screen print.

Claudia Linder McCann.

She felt sick. Even though she'd expected that it was her stepmother, she'd held out hope that she was wrong, that she wasn't going to have to tell her father that the woman he loved was likely a traitor to the country he loved.

When she'd seen enough, she shut down the system and put the flash drive back in her coat pocket.

When she got back to the kitchen, Ethan was there. No one was talking.

Ethan raised his head. "Claudia?"

She nodded. "I'd like to tell my father before going to the authorities. What about them?"

"We leave them for now. They aren't going anywhere." Ethan opened a cupboard door, reached in and pulled out two glasses. He filled each with water. Then he reached into one of the drawers under the open counter where a package of straws was clearly visible.

He put a straw in each glass and sat one in front of

each man. "I'm not going to put tape over your mouths. That way, if you get thirsty and you're real careful, you should be able to lean forward and get yourself a drink. Pace yourself because it will likely be a few hours before someone comes back for you."

Dad was looking down. Ted still had his chin up. "Maybe we won't be here when you come back," he said, his tone belligerent.

"You'll be here," Ethan said confidently. "Now, you can yell and scream and maybe get the attention of your neighbors. But then you're going to have a whole lot of explaining to do. I don't think your dad thinks that's a good idea and right now, I think you better listen to him. This ends now."

Dad raised his head and gave Ethan a brief nod.

"For what it's worth," Ethan said, his voice soft, "I had nothing to do with Trevor's death. I am more sorry than you could ever imagine that it happened. And if information was truly leaked, I promise you that I would kill the man who was responsible if I knew who it was. But I can assure you, it wasn't me."

Neither man said anything in response but Chandler could see tears well up in Ted's eyes. War had taken his brother and in the middle of the night, he'd seen a way to make some small amend. No matter how unhinged it might be.

"We should go," she said.

The only transportation they had available to them was Ted's Buick. They got in, Ethan driving, Chandler in the passenger seat.

"I guess I owe you some explanation," he said.

She studied him. "I think I've got it mostly figured out."

"I want you to know it all. You deserve that. I did retire from the military. But something happened before I left, something bad, and there are people who think it was my fault."

"What happened?"

"Eight soldiers were killed. Four on the ground and we lost two helicopters, with two men each. Our pilots had been doing surveillance for weeks. We were confident that we'd identified a stronghold for a terrorist cell that had successfully eluded us since the beginning of the war. Everything was planned perfectly."

"But something went wrong?" she asked.

"They were waiting for us. With more firepower than we could ever have anticipated. At first I thought they just got lucky. But as the weeks went by and more intelligence filtered in, it became apparent that they'd known we were coming. Somebody had sold us out."

"Not you."

"No. But there was some damning evidence. They believed I had made radio transmissions to the enemy."

"I don't understand."

"I didn't either. But they produced a tape of my voice giving details of the mission. There were enemy combatants on the other end."

"I can't believe… How is that even possible?"

"It was a fake. I told them that. But you can imagine that they found it difficult to believe."

"How did you prove your innocence?"

"There had only been a few times that I had discussed the mission and that was with those who had a need to know. It was with a handful of trusted pilots. I was always very careful when relaying highly classified information. I remembered exactly what I'd said and when I'd said it. I told the investigators and they ultimately got independent verification that supported the wild idea that somehow snippets of those different conversations got recorded and used to made me look like the bad guy."

"Once you told them what had happened, did they identify who might have done it?"

"No."

"So you still don't know?"

"I don't. I couldn't imagine any of the men I told doing such a horrible thing. These were men I'd flown with for years. I think it was someone else entirely. Maybe something as simple as someone bugged the area where the conversations occurred. Then they had the skill and ability to weave two different conversations into one and feed in appropriate responses on the part of the enemy."

"It sounds very complicated."

"You're telling me. Complicated. Insane. That's the only explanation I came up with. It could be one of a thousand-plus soldiers who were assigned under that command."

She looked at him with tears in her eyes. "That must have been so frustrating for you."

"Frustrating. Maddening. Scary."

"Well, it's a crazy story and a crazy situation but I can't imagine anyone ever thinking that you could do something like that. It just wouldn't happen."

Warmth flooded back into his cold body. He'd been so afraid that he'd see speculation in her pretty eyes, that he'd be able to sense the change in her posture. That her trust in him was broken.

But there was none of that. "I wish everybody accepted the explanation as easily as that," he said.

"They don't know you as well as I do."

"We haven't seen each other for more than fifteen years," he reminded her. "People change."

"They do. And people hide things well. I know that better than most. But what I also know is that you've been a good person since you were a boy. I remember how you used to look out for your mom. Even as a kid, you knew that she shouldn't be walking home from work in the dark alone and you made sure she never did. And remember the summer that Brody broke his leg? You made sure that he didn't get left out of anything. You figured out a way that he could participate in whatever you and Mack were doing even when it would have been much easier to leave him sitting on the couch. You were a kid but you knew the right thing to do."

He didn't know what to say.

It didn't matter because she wasn't done. "You want to know the reason that Christivo's deception really hurt me? Because my dad had drummed it into my head that the most important quality a person can have is personal integrity. He said that many times people do the right thing because they don't want to be caught doing the wrong thing. But he said there are people who do the right thing because it's the only possibility that they see for themselves. They're honorable. And whenever he would talk about this, he'd always use you as the example. 'Ethan Moore,' he used to say. 'Now that's a kid who's got a personal code that he lives by.' That's why I could never tell anybody about Christivo. I couldn't let them know that I'd chosen somebody who had no personal code of honor. What did that make me? Someone with no judgment? Even worse, someone who didn't value integrity? Or, God forbid, maybe even someone who had no integrity of her own because she was willing to settle for a lack of it in others."

"No, Chandler. You're none of those things." It made him crazy that she would even think that way. "You have integrity. Otherwise, you'd have reported this whole mess to the authorities and let them sort it out. But you knew that it was possible that your stepmother could be innocent and you didn't want to damage her reputation or your relationship with her. Most of all, you didn't want to hurt your father. That's integrity. And honor. And courage. And sacrifice. And—"

"Enough," she said, smiling. "I get your point."

He reached for her and his mouth settled on hers. All the pent-up emotion of the past hour seemed to surge through him and he kissed her with a fierceness that bordered out of control.

When he finally came up for air, she giggled. "We're still in Ted's garage."

"I know," he said. "But I couldn't go one more minute without tasting you." There was so much more that he wanted to tell her. But not sitting in Ted Matchmore's car in his garage with things still unsettled with Claudia Linder McCann.

"Let's finish this," he said. He pushed the button to raise the garage door. "We need to get my truck and then go to your Dad's house."

"I just hope I don't run into Claudia there."

"If she thinks the gig is up, maybe she'll be lawyering up, getting ready to defend herself against an investigation."

"Not yet. Once security would have contacted her, I think she'd have wanted to be on-site. The one thing I've learned about her is that she's a control freak. She doesn't have the technical skill to do this but she'd have called one of the other computer specialists in to run a report on who had accessed the system at approximately three-thirty and what they looked at."

"Why? She has to know it was you."

"She probably suspects but I don't think she could be a hundred percent confident. First of all, there's probably still some doubt that I escaped the crash and the fire. With all the snow, I doubt they've had time to say that the search has been exhausted. Even if they have, she'd have to believe that I somehow managed to cross the mountains and get to Denver in one of the worst blizzards in the past ten years. She'll ask for a description from the guard and he's not going to be able to tell her much. He barely saw me and I had my hair up underneath Lauren's hat and I had on her jacket. I used my user test sign-on and quite frankly, I don't think there's any record of who that sign-on belongs to."

"You're pretty smart," he said. "A good thinker. I like that."

She smiled at him. "Why, thank you."

"Let's go," he said. "I hate driving this car. And Molly is probably in desperate need of a fire hydrant."

MOLLY, THE GOOD and practical dog she was, was sleeping. She raised her head when they got in, looked at both Ethan and Chandler and smiled. At least Chandler thought it looked like a smile. "You're such a good girl," she told the dog, framing Molly's pretty face in her hands. "I was worried about you."

"Doesn't appear as if she was terribly concerned about us," Ethan said drily. "I'll remember that the next time she wants to go out at two in the morning."

"Don't pay any attention to him," Chandler cooed. "I'll take you out any time of night you need me to."

The minute she said it, she regretted it. It was a bit presumptuous. "I'm sorry," she added quickly. "I'm not sure why that came out that way."

He stared at her. The tips of his ears were a soft pink. "When this is over, we need to talk. I'm not going to have this conversation on a busy street, in a pickup truck that quite frankly smells a little bit like a dog who has a gas problem."

It was a small reprieve, but he was right. They had to confront a traitor.

BAKER AND CLAUDIA LINDER MCCANN had bought themselves a big house. The house the McCanns had had on Walnut Street had been nice. All the houses in that affluent neighborhood had been. His mother used to complain about all the bathrooms that rich people had to have. By the looks of this house, one might need all their fingers and toes to do an accurate bathroom count. While it wasn't any of his business, Ethan couldn't help but think that this house, even located in a subdivision of really showy houses, looked a bit over-the-top.

"Pillars?" he asked.

"Claudia's favorite movie is *Gone With the Wind.* Welcome to Denver's Tara."

It just didn't look like Baker McCann.

"What if your dad isn't here?" Ethan asked. "He may have gone west, to join the search-and-rescue efforts."

"He would have wanted to. It's possible that he found a way to get there just as we found a way to get back.

If he's not here, I'm going to have to call him. I'd rather tell him in person but there's no time."

"So we ring the doorbell?"

She shook her head. "Claudia may be here. I want us to enter the house very carefully. If we go through the garage, we can enter through the back hallway. My dad spends most of his time in his study, which is toward the back of the house."

"But how are we going to get into the garage?"

She picked up her dirty jeans, which were still on the floor of the truck. Molly had been using them off and on as a bed. She reached into the pocket and pulled out her key ring with the two keys. "One was for the cabin and the other for this house. Dad gave it to me when I had to water their plants when they were on a trip. It unlocks any door. If the security alarm goes off, I know the code."

It sounded simple enough. Enter through the garage, either find Baker McCann or call him, tell him what was going on and together, identify next steps. "Okay. If the way to this garage door is via the backyard, I'm going to park my truck on the street behind the house. No need to advertise our presence by pulling in the driveway."

He made a turn at the next corner, judged the distance and pulled his truck off to the side of the road. These residential streets had not been plowed as well as the city business district but he got as close to the curb as he could. "Even with your boots, your feet are going to get wet," he said. "The snow in the backyard is probably a foot deep."

"It doesn't matter," she said. "All I can think about is how devastated my dad is going to be."

"He's going to be elated that you're alive," Ethan reminded her.

"I hope that's enough," Chandler said, getting out of the truck.

They stuck to the tree line as they approached the house. Chandler used her key to enter the garage. It was mostly dark inside the empty garage, although windows on the far side provided enough light that Ethan could tell that there would have been room for three cars if Baker didn't have his lawn mower and snowblower taking up one spot.

They brushed the snow off their pants as best they could. Chandler reached for the door connecting the garage to the house, but hesitated before turning the knob.

"What's wrong?" Ethan whispered.

"This is the hardest thing I've ever had to do," she said. "Once he gets past being angry, my dad is going to feel like a fool for trusting Claudia. I'd do anything to prevent that."

"I know. And *he* will know, too. That's what will ultimately help him."

She turned the knob. The door opened without a sound. No alarm rang. It was a wide hallway with ceramic tile that was dark and rich-looking. The walls were painted a pale green and there was framed artwork on both sides.

If the back hallway was any indication, the house was every bit as impressive inside as it was outside. But still, he wasn't getting the feel of Baker McCann, who'd seemed quite at home sleeping on a sofa bed in a small cabin.

Chandler motioned for him to continue down the hallway. Ethan had taken four steps when a dark figure stepped out of a doorway, wrapped a strong forearm around his neck and yanked him back.

"You've got five seconds to tell me what the hell is going on."

Chapter Sixteen

Ethan hadn't talked to his friend in more than a year but he'd have recognized Mack's voice anywhere. "Hard to do if I can't breathe," he said.

Mack let go. Ethan turned to face him but he was already focused on his sister. "Hey, Cat-Eyes," Mack said, hugging his sister hard. He didn't let go for a very long time. When he finally pulled back, he added, "Nice to see you."

Chandler had tears in her eyes. "I'm sorry," she said. "I didn't mean to worry you."

Mack shook his head. "It's okay. It's not a good day when you hear that your sister's car has been found in some trees. With the explosion at the cabin, I knew something was terribly wrong. Unfortunately, I was on the other side of the world and it took a little finagling to get here. I was on a plane when you called. Once I landed, I tried you but you didn't answer. That didn't make me very happy."

She pulled her phone out of her pocket. Ethan looked at the screen. Two missed calls. Both from Mack's number. "I'm sorry," Chandler said. "It was on silent. I didn't think to check that. I never put my own phone on silent."

Ted Matchmore had probably put it on silent when he'd been playing with her phone.

"I'll forgive you this time, Cat-Eyes."

Mack turned his attention to Ethan and pulled him into a rough hug. "I owe you," he said.

Maybe now wasn't the time to tell Mack that he'd spent a good portion of the past day and a half in bed with his sister. "You don't owe me," he said simply.

But Chandler wasn't having any of that. "He saved my life. Not once. A couple times. I wouldn't have made it without him."

There was more than gratitude in her voice. Respect. Admiration. Maybe something bigger. It made him warm and when he saw Mack's eyes narrow, he knew that his friend had picked up on it, as well.

"Ethan?" He reached out a hand, caught Ethan's shoulder. Held it tight.

"Later." If Mack wanted to get in his face about Ethan's taking advantage of Chandler when she was in a vulnerable state, he was going to have to wait. Now they needed to find Baker McCann before Claudia Linder McCann decided to have any more of her goons start shooting.

"Where's Dad?" Chandler asked, once again tracking closely with him.

Mack looked between the two of them and evidently decided to halt his inquisition. It was probably what made him a super secret agent—he had the ability to interpret, assimilate and respond quickly and appropriately.

That, however, did not keep him from giving Ethan's shoulder a vicious squeeze before he let go.

"On his way back," Mack said. "Should be here in

about an hour, maybe less. He took off for the cabin when he got the call from the Colorado State Patrol very early yesterday morning. Hardly any commercial flights were going but he chartered a plane. I was going to meet him at the cabin but he texted me several hours ago and said to come here and wait. I've only been here about twenty minutes."

"Have you seen Claudia?" Chandler asked.

Mack shook his head. "Nope. That was a relief."

Ethan stepped forward. "We should let your dad know that Chandler is safe."

Mack smiled. "It appears that all those years ago, we weren't as smart as we thought we were. Dad knows the code. Has always known the code. When he saw the books, he put two and two together. That's why he's coming home."

"Did he tell anyone besides you?" Ethan asked.

"I doubt it. They had already suspended the search. The weather in Denver isn't bad but it's still snowing and blowing in the mountains."

"Did he tell Claudia?" Chandler asked, her tone worried.

Mack shrugged. "I don't know, Cat-Eyes. She's his wife, so probably. What's the big deal?"

Chandler took a big breath and launched into the whole story. She did, however, leave out the part about Ted Matchmore and their brief capture. No need to pile more drama on top of drama. Not at this point.

Mack listened carefully, never interrupting.

When Chandler finished, she said, "I'm turning Claudia in. It's going to ruin the company and I'm sorry for all the people who are going to lose their jobs because of her greed, but I can't worry about that right now. I want to tell Dad first."

"Good call." Mack looked at his watch. "I hope to hell he hurries. Claudia is a wild card. No telling what she's thinking."

"Agreed," Chandler said.

"Come with me. We'll watch the front," Mack said.

Chandler shook her head. "I'm staying with Ethan."

Mack gave Ethan a long look before turning and leaving the room.

"He knows," Chandler said.

Ethan nodded. "If he wasn't sure, he is now. I'm not confident that he's happy."

"I'm his little sister. It's always been his job to protect me, especially after Mom died and Dad was so distraught. He just needs a minute to accept that somebody else has taken over his responsibilities. Plus, you've always been his best friend. He sees you in that role. Not necessarily with me."

With her. He wanted that more than anything. And when this was all over, he was going to tell her.

He leaned forward and kissed her hard. When he finally pulled back, she was smiling. He grabbed her hand. "Your dad will be home soon and this whole thing will be over with."

"A federal investigation is long and ugly and it may get worse before it gets better," she warned. "They're going to want to question my dad, want to know what he knew."

"Baker McCann is one of the toughest guys I know. He'll get through this. You all will."

"I hope you're right."

It was fifteen minutes later when they heard the sound of an approaching car.

"Dad," Mack called out.

Ethan gripped her hand. "Ready?" he asked her.

As ready as she ever would be. She heard the overhead garage door open, then close. Then the interior door. Footsteps.

When Baker McCann rounded the corner, she wanted to launch herself into his arms and to hold him tight. But she stayed in place. She was about to hurt him badly.

Her father saw Mack first. Then his eyes moved, taking in Ethan in the corner, resting only a second, before settling on her. "Chandler," he said, his voice soft.

"Daddy." She hadn't called him that since she was a little girl but somehow, it felt right.

He spread his arms and suddenly she was in them. This man, who had been both mother and father for so many years, had always been her rock. That was why the chill that had crept into their relationship after Claudia's arrival had been so difficult.

"I'm sorry," she said, her face against his shirt.

He patted her back. "It's okay, honey. Everything is okay now." He rocked her for a moment, his big body swaying. Finally, he pulled back. "What the hell happened, Chandler?"

"I have something to tell you," she said. "I…" She looked at Mack, then at Ethan, who gave her an encouraging nod. "This is going to be hard to believe but I know what I'm talking about. Information was leaked from Linder Automation. About one of our most secret weapons. It was sold, Daddy."

"Who?" he demanded.

"Claudia," she whispered.

Her dad dropped his hands and took a step back. "That's a horrible allegation, Chandler. Look, I know Claudia isn't your favorite—"

"Dad, I'm sorry," Chandler tried again.

"There has to be some mistake," her dad said. "Claudia would never do that. You've just never been able to see the good in her."

Chandler could feel her heart squeeze tight. He didn't believe her.

Ethan stepped forward and rested his hand across her lower back. Offering support. Trust. Resilience. "She's not wrong, Baker. Chandler has done everything she could possibly do to ensure that what she's telling you is correct. She almost died a couple times for her efforts. She would rather it wasn't Claudia. But all evidence suggests it is."

Baker looked at Ethan with hostility in his eyes.

Ethan didn't flinch and he held her dad's stare. If Chandler hadn't loved him before, she loved him then. Ethan thought the world of Baker McCann. And he was risking all of that to support her.

"Just please listen to her, Baker." He turned to her. "Tell him, Chandler. Tell him what you know."

And Chandler went through the whole thing again for the second time in the past hour. When she told her dad about the car deliberately bumping her and sending her over the edge of the mountains, Ethan could see the veins in the big man's neck stick out. When she talked about how close she'd come to being inside the cabin when it exploded, Baker grabbed the counter for support. And finally, when she told him about the security guard shooting at her, Baker sat down hard on a kitchen chair.

As Mack had done, Baker listened carefully, never

interrupting. When she finished her story, the kitchen was very quiet.

After a long minute, Mack stepped forward. "We need to get to the authorities and let them sort this out."

"Agreed," Ethan said.

Mack looked at his watch. "I left a very sticky situation in South America. I need to go back now that I know Chandler is safe." He turned to stare at Ethan. "You got this?"

"I got it," Ethan said.

"Don't screw it up," Mack said.

Ethan knew he wasn't talking about the investigation. "I won't."

Mack walked over and kissed Chandler on the cheek. He leaned close to her ear but spoke just loudly enough that Ethan could hear. "You could have done worse, Cat-Eyes. Much worse."

"Thank you," she whispered.

Then Mack gave Baker a hard hug. "Trust Ethan and Chandler, Dad. As much as it hurts, trust them. I'll be back as soon as I can. We'll rebuild the cabin. We'll do it together."

Her dad didn't say anything but he did hug Mack and roughly pat his back.

Then Mack left, closing the door softly behind him. Again, the silence was deafening.

"I've got my dog in my truck," Ethan said. "I'm going to let her out and feed her." Before he left the room, he leaned close to her. "You did great. He loves you. He just needs a minute." He walked out the way they'd entered the house.

Chandler studied her father. He looked old and weary and she knew that her announcement had shaken him to his core. But she also knew that Ethan's quiet proclamation of support and Mack's insistence that she and Ethan were right had sealed the deal.

"I should have known something was wrong," he said, his voice soft. "I was so worried when I heard the news of the accident. And Claudia seemed as concerned. But then, when I was told about the cabin, and I was trying to fit the pieces together, Claudia was insistent that the two events didn't have anything to do with each other. When I told her that I needed to be in the mountains, I wanted her to come with me. She said that she couldn't, that she absolutely had to be at work for the next several days. Her work has always been important to her but I have to admit, I needed her."

"Oh, Daddy," Chandler said. Baker McCann had been disappointed on so many levels.

"When I got to Crow Hollow," he added, "and I realized that you were still alive and with Ethan, I was ecstatic. When I told Claudia, she said all the right things but I could tell that something was wrong."

Her dad's words sunk in. "Claudia knows that I'm alive and with Ethan?"

"Yes, and it wasn't the best news I've had lately," a female voice said.

Chandler whirled. Claudia stood in the doorway, her arm extended. She had a gun pointed directly at Chandler.

"You're a pain in the ass, Chandler," she said. She had an ugly smile on her severe-looking face.

"I'd rather be a pain in the ass than a traitor to my country."

Her stepmother shrugged. "This has become unnecessarily complicated. I knew you would run to that damn cabin that your father was always wanting me to visit. You should have died there. Those fools should have made sure you were inside rather than assuming that you'd died in the crash."

"You should hire better help."

Again Claudia shrugged. "Not my help. My customer's help. They could mobilize more quickly than I could. So incompetent, though. It's a wonder if they'll even be smart enough to use the technology that I sold them."

She was so proud, so brazen about her actions, that Chandler wanted to scratch her eyes out. But what she wanted most was to stop this before it went any further. Certainly before Ethan returned to the house and got caught in the cross fire.

"It's over, Claudia. Mack knows. He just left. Even if you kill me and Daddy, Mack will tell everyone."

Claudia's eyes flared with anger. "I can handle your brother, Cat-Eyes. That's what he calls you, right? Well, I think you just used up all nine of your lives." She put her finger on the trigger.

Chapter Seventeen

As Ethan pulled his truck into Baker McCann's driveway, he kept one hand on the wheel and used the other to pet Molly. "Got to go?" he asked the dog.

She barked in response.

He opened the door and before he could catch her, she'd leaped from the truck and was headed for the side of the house, opposite of the garage. "Molly," he said under his breath. They didn't have time to fool around. He followed her around the corner of the house and saw her squatting near a big pine tree that hugged the house.

He waited and looked around. The McCanns had at least an acre of yard. With all the fresh snow, it was beautiful. Untouched.

Except there were fresh footprints leading up to a side door. He got close. Small footprints. Pointed toe. Women's shoes.

His vision narrowed.

He pulled his gun and turned the handle of the door. It opened. There was a laundry room on one side, a bath on the other. Making no sound, he ran toward the back of the house. When he got close to the kitchen, he heard Baker.

"Don't do it, Claudia. It's over."

He heard a shrill laugh. "You're wrong, Baker. Your son can throw around all the ugly accusations that he wants. I've covered my trail. It's a shame that you won't be around to spend the money."

"We had plenty of money, Claudia," Baker said.

The woman laughed again. "You know what they say, darling. You can never be too rich or too thin. It doesn't matter, anyway. It's too late. It was too late once I'd accepted the first payment. My customers aren't exactly the type that you suddenly decide to stop doing business with."

Ethan took another two steps. Saw the gun in her hand.

Saw her finger move.

Ethan shot her. The bullet caught her in the shoulder and she fell sideways, knocking into the wall. She dropped the gun and Ethan moved fast to secure it but Baker beat him to it. The man picked up the gun and with absolutely still hands, pointed it at his wife. She was clenching her right shoulder with her left hand, half sitting up, her skinny body propped up by the dark wood that framed the doorway.

Baker pulled his cell phone off his belt and dialed a few numbers. "We need the police and we need an ambulance," he said.

Ethan pulled Chandler into his arms. He buried his face in her hair and filled his lungs with her scent. She was alive. And she was his.

He wasn't wasting one more minute. "Chandler, marry me," he said. "I love you. I will always love you."

She lifted her face. There were tears in her beautiful eyes. "I'm losing track of how many times you've saved me," she said.

He shook his head. "You saved me," he said.

"I cheat at poker," she said.

"I'm counting on that."

"I get cranky when I have to share my desserts."

"Won't ever happen," he said. "We'll always order two."

"I'm going to let Molly sleep on the bed."

"Whatever."

She kissed him. "Yes."

"Yes, what?" he asked, his heart flooded with hope.

"Yes, I'll marry you. I've loved you forever, Ethan Moore. It's about time you noticed."

* * * * *

STALKED, the second book in Beverly Long's miniseries THE MEN OF CROW HOLLOW, is available next month. Look for it wherever Harlequin Intrigue books are sold!

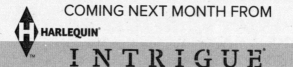

COMING NEXT MONTH FROM

HARLEQUIN

INTRIGUE

Available August 19, 2014

#1515 MAVERICK SHERIFF
Sweetwater Ranch • by Delores Fossen
Thrown into a dangerous investigation, Sheriff Cooper McKinnon and Assistant District Attorney Jessa Wells must join forces to protect the baby they each claim as their own.

#1516 WAY OF THE SHADOWS
Shadow Agents: Guts and Glory • by Cynthia Eden
FBI profiler Noelle Evers can't remember him...but former army ranger Thomas Anthony would kill in order to protect the one woman he can't live without. With Noelle once again in a predator's sights, can Thomas save the woman he loves a second time?

#1517 DEAD MAN'S CURVE
The Gates • by Paula Graves
When CIA double agent Sinclair Solano is lured out of hiding to recover his kidnapped sister, he crosses swords with a beautiful FBI agent, Ava Trent, who wants him—dead or alive.

#1518 THE WHARF
Brody Law • by Carol Ericson
Police Chief Ryan Brody trusts true-crime writer Kacie Manning to help him catch a killer, but Kacie is keeping a dark secret from him. Can Kacie abandon her quest for revenge to give their love a chance...or will the *real* psychopath get to her first?

#1519 SNOW BLIND
by Cassie Miles
After witnessing a murder, Sasha Campbell turns to local sheriff's deputy Brady Ellis for protection. But while Brady and Sasha grow closer to one another, the killer gets dangerously closer to them.

#1520 STALKED
The Men from Crow Hollow • by Beverly Long
Tabloid celebrity Hope Minnow believes recent death threats are a publicity stunt and refuses navy intelligence officer turned bodyguard Mack McCann's protection. But when the threats turn very real, can Mack get to Hope in time to save her?

YOU CAN FIND MORE INFORMATION ON UPCOMING HARLEQUIN® TITLES,
FREE EXCERPTS AND MORE AT WWW.HARLEQUIN.COM.

HICNM0814

REQUEST YOUR FREE BOOKS!
2 FREE NOVELS PLUS 2 FREE GIFTS!

✦HARLEQUIN®

INTRIGUE®

BREATHTAKING ROMANTIC SUSPENSE

YES! Please send me 2 FREE Harlequin Intrigue® novels and my 2 FREE gifts (gifts are worth about $10). After receiving them, if I don't wish to receive any more books, I can return the shipping statement marked "cancel." If I don't cancel, I will receive 6 brand-new novels every month and be billed just $4.74 per book in the U.S. or $5.24 per book in Canada. That's a savings of at least 14% off the cover price! It's quite a bargain! Shipping and handling is just 50¢ per book in the U.S. and 75¢ per book in Canada.* I understand that accepting the 2 free books and gifts places me under no obligation to buy anything. I can always return a shipment and cancel at any time. Even if I never buy another book, the two free books and gifts are mine to keep forever.

182/382 HDN F42N

Name	(PLEASE PRINT)
Address	Apt. #
City	State/Prov.	Zip/Postal Code

Signature (if under 18, a parent or guardian must sign)

Mail to the Harlequin® Reader Service:
IN U.S.A.: P.O. Box 1867, Buffalo, NY 14240-1867
IN CANADA: P.O. Box 609, Fort Erie, Ontario L2A 5X3

**Are you a subscriber to Harlequin Intrigue books
and want to receive the larger-print edition?
Call 1-800-873-8635 or visit www.ReaderService.com.**

* Terms and prices subject to change without notice. Prices do not include applicable taxes. Sales tax applicable in N.Y. Canadian residents will be charged applicable taxes. Offer not valid in Quebec. This offer is limited to one order per household. Not valid for current subscribers to Harlequin Intrigue books. All orders subject to credit approval. Credit or debit balances in a customer's account(s) may be offset by any other outstanding balance owed by or to the customer. Please allow 4 to 6 weeks for delivery. Offer available while quantities last.

Your Privacy—The Harlequin® Reader Service is committed to protecting your privacy. Our Privacy Policy is available online at www.ReaderService.com or upon request from the Harlequin Reader Service.

We make a portion of our mailing list available to reputable third parties that offer products we believe may interest you. If you prefer that we not exchange your name with third parties, or if you wish to clarify or modify your communication preferences, please visit us at www.ReaderService.com/consumerchoice or write to us at Harlequin Reader Service Preference Service, P.O. Box 9062, Buffalo, NY 14269. Include your complete name and address.

HI13R

"You had my son's DNA tested, why?" Jessa demanded.
But that was as far as she got. Her chest started pumping
as if starved for air, and she dropped back and let the now
closed door support her.

The dark circles under her eyes let him know she hadn't
been sleeping.

Neither had he.

It'd taken every ounce of willpower for him not to rush
back to the hospital to get a better look at the little boy.

"How's Liam?" he asked.

She glared at him for so long that Cooper wasn't sure
she'd answer. "He's better, but you already know that. You've
called at least a dozen times checking on his condition."

He had. Cooper also knew Liam was doing so well that
he'd probably be released from the hospital tomorrow.

"He'll make a full recovery?" Cooper asked.

Again, she glared. "Yes. In fact, he already wants to get
up and run around. Now, why?" she added without pausing.

Cooper pulled in a long breath that he would need and
sank down on the edge of his desk. "Because of the blood
type match. And because we never found my son's body."

Even though she'd no doubt already come up with that

answer, Jessa huffed and threw her hands in the air. "And what? You think I found him on the riverbank and pretended to adopt him? Well, I didn't, and Liam's not your son. I want you to put a stop to that DNA test."

Cooper shook his head. "If you're sure he's not my son, then the test will come back as no match."

Her glare got worse. "You're doing this to get back at me." Her breath broke, and the tears came.

Oh, man.

He didn't want this. Not with both of them already emotional wrecks. They were both powder kegs right now, and the flames were shooting all around them. Still, he went closer, and because all those emotions had apparently made him dumber than dirt, Cooper slipped his arm around her.

She fought him. Of course. Jessa clearly didn't want his comfort, sympathy or anything else other than an assurance to put a stop to that test. Still, he held on despite her fists pushing against his chest. One more ragged sob, however, and she sagged against him.

There it was again. That tug deep down in his body. Yeah, dumber than dirt, all right. His body just didn't seem to understand that an attractive woman in his arms could mean nothing.

Even when Jessa looked up at him.

That tug tugged a little harder. Because, yeah, she was attractive, and if the investigation and accusations hadn't cropped up, he might have considered asking her out.

So much for that plan.

Find out what happens next in
MAVERICK SHERIFF
by USA TODAY bestselling author Delores Fossen,
available September 2014, only from
Harlequin® Intrigue®.

HIEXP69782